Tina's Story
Life of an Addict

Author Andre Glover

www.AndreGloverProductions.com

PUBLISHER'S NOTE:

This book is a work of fiction. Names, Characters, places and incidents are products of the imagination. Or used fictitiously any resemblance to actual events or locals or persons living or dead, is entirely coincidental.

Copyright © 2016 Andre Glover

All Rights Reserved, including the right of reproduction in whole or in part of any form.

ISBN-13: 978-0-692-03249-7

Library of Congress Catalog Card Number: In publication data.

Life of an Addict: Tina's Story

Written by: Andre Glover

Edited by: Complete Steps Publishing, LLC

Text Formation: Complete Steps Publishing, LLC

Cover Design and Layout: Dynasty's Cover Me

Printed in the United States of America

DEDICATION

I dedicate this book to my children Andre' Glover Jr. and Yashica Glover. I want you to know that I love you two dearly. To my Aunt Cennie Kendall and my Grandma Carrie Kendall, I love you and miss you. May you continue to Rest in Peace.

ACKNOWLEDGEMENT

To my beautiful mother Etta Glover, you raised me to become the man that I am today. I thank you for all that you have done for me over the years. My loving father and stepmother, Leon and Lillie Robinson, I appreciate the love you have shown me. I will cherish that forever. To my sister Sherita Glover, you have always believed in me. Look at me now sis. To my brother Bobby Glover, who rides for me even when the wheels fell off, you were there. I thank you for that. To my sisters Holly and Alicia Robinson, who look up to me I love you for life. To my loving and caring nieces Chiquita, Shequala and Christina and my smooth nephew, Jonquil. I love you more than you will ever know. To all my friends and family who prayed for me, especially my nieces and nephew. I thank you for the uplifting during my time of need. To Complete Steps Publishing, thank you for making my vision come to life. To the special lady in my life Keshia Marshall, I love you baby and thank you for holding me down. When I wanted to buy shoes you said get this book done. But most of all I have to thank my Lord and Savior Jesus Christ without You I am nothing.

INTRODUCTION

There are many people in the world who struggle with drinking and drugging. But we need to understand that God can use anybody to deliver a message. This book was written in 2005 and now you can finally enjoy the story I have written. Drugs do not discriminate. It does not matter whether you are black, white or Hispanic. It does not matter whether you are young or old. We can all become a victim like the young Tina you are about to read about. Blacks has the highest cases of HIV/AIDS due to many factors and of course the exchange of unprotected sex for drugs. Many are between the ages of 28-42. Make it a priority to learn the facts on how to stay HIV negative and resourceful on how to manage your care if you are positive. Please protect yourself by having the necessary conversations, proper use of condoms and saying no to drugs.

Welcome to Tina's Story,

Author Andre Glover

CHAPTER 1

It was the year 1987, when a young 18-year-old Tina walked across the stage at her high school graduation. An honor student, a vivacious cheerleader, nominated and voted prom queen. This moment made the happiest time in her life. After receiving her diploma of completion with honors, Tina decided to attend the graduation party of the year at Brian's house. Brian a football player and Tina's ex-boyfriend was having the event of the year to celebrate a major milestone in their lives. Everybody who was somebody was at the party. The party was wall to wall with ecstatic young adults all holding Solo Cups with something in it warming their blood. As Tina sashayed through the crowd, Paul a handsome graduate grabbed her by the waist.

"Would you like to dance beautiful?" Tina with a bright smile on her face softly replied, "Yes." After their dance Paul who is also a friend of Brian looks into her eyes.

"Would you like something to drink?"

"Maybe a small shot of gin and juice."

By this time Tina's friend Sheila approached the both of them. Sheila is Tina's best friend. They have known one another since kindergarten. Sheila was on the wild side. She loved to drink, smoke weed and have sex.

"Girl it's graduation night. You have to smoke a joint with me tonight." Sheila thundered.

"Maybe later." Tina whispered. Tina had never smoked anything in her life. But then again in the back of her mind she was thinking, what the hell it's graduation. By then Paul had returned with the drinks. Paul was a handsome fella. Tina never paid any attention towards him. Paul had a crush on Tina for some time. However, he never told anyone because she had dated Brian.

"Nice party." A smiling Tina expressed to Brian. As she smells the aroma of Gin coming from her cup they begin to walk over by the stairs. Paul starts probing Tina about what was next in her life.

"Now that school is out what are your plans?"

"I like to do hair," Tina said. "So I am going to try to attend a beauty   school here in Charlotte." Tina was eight years old when her Mother died. She was raised by her Grandmother. Her Father was in prison doing 25 years for selling drugs.

"I will probably just get a job and live on my own," Tina added.

"What are your plans Paul?" "I don't know yet" as he turns up his cup of Gin with no chaser. "I never told anyone this but I always thought you were the most beautiful girl in the school."

"Excuse me." Was coming from the party animal Sheila. She walks over with Ice Man, a former lover with a joint in hand.

"Now it's time to blaze." Ice Man was the schools' hot boy. He is known around town for having the best powder and weed. He is always dressed to impress and drove a 1982 candy apple red, convertible Ford Mustang.

"Here you, fire it up," as Sheila passes the joint to Tina. "Huh! Huh! Fire it up!" Tina began to choke as she inhales. Everyone laughs as they pass the joint around. Then they all went on the dance floor for a while.

"Would you like another drink?" Paul asked.

"Why not?" Tina said. As the night grew young everybody was beyond the wilding out stage, so Ice Man asked the crew,

"Do you guys want to go for a ride?"

"Why not, this party is getting out of hand." Tina said. Ice Man, Sheila, Paul and Tina roll out. At 1:15 AM they were riding around the city and Prince's song 'Do Me Baby' came on the radio. Sheila wanted the radio turned up. Sheila had begun rolling up another joint as she asked the others if they were down for one more. Ice Man slips a pint of Paul Mason from under the passenger seat and pulls over to a nearby park. They all get out the car to smoke and drink. Paul pulls Tina to the back of the car and they start kissing and touching one another while Ice Man and Sheila sing to Prince. Around 2 AM, Ice Man and the crew got back in the car for another ride. This time they stop at one of his friend's house, B-Money. A big time dope dealer from the Westside. He left Ice Man the keys to his place while he was out of town to take care of some business. B-Money was older. He was 24 and rolling in dough. He's the guy Ice Man sold dope for. As they entered the house Ice Man turns on some music.

"Make yourselves at home," as he grabs Sheila by the hand leading her to the bedroom. He lays her on the bed and starts kissing her. He takes his hands and softly pulls her skirt up and rubs her hairy vagina as he gently sucks the nipples of her small breast. Then he pulls her head towards his big penis. Sheila licks the head and stroking his shaft like a pro. He shoves her on the bed and penetrates his penis in her wetness.

She screams, "Oh God! Fuck Me! Oh God, Fuck Me!" He turns her around and lifts her round juicy ass up in the air as he puts his penis back inside of her vagina, plunging it in and out. Sheila grabs the pillow and pulls it to her face to camouflage her screams. Yet, her screams grew louder and louder. He flips her around on her back and reinserts himself inside of her moistness as he pulls himself closer to her.

"I still love you," she whispers.

"I know," replying in a panting voice. They kiss as Ice Man makes his way down towards her twitching vagina. Sheila moans and groans while Ice Man sucks her out of her mind. He comes up for air and sticks his big penis back in her as he relaxes her legs over his shoulders. Sheila screams as tears roll down her face. Her vagina was talking back as she climaxes all over his penis. Two minutes afterwards he bust inside of her and cum rolls down between her ass cheeks onto the bed. Both of them out of breath, cuddled up and the pillow talk about their previous relationship begins. Meanwhile back in the living room. Paul and Tina had made a pallet on the floor out of blankets and sheets they had found in the closet. The carpet was soft and plush under the bundle of covers, which made it even more comfortable when they lay down. Tina was very nervous because she knew what Paul wanted and she was not sure if she was ready to give it up. She had only had sex once and that was with Brian over a year ago. As they began conversation, Tina found Paul's hand rubbing her tender thighs. She got hot and bothered by the feeling her body was receiving from his touches.

Reassuring it was okay, Paul says to Tina, "Relax, you," he softly whispers as he unbuttons her blouse and seductively kisses her neck.

"Do you have a condom?"

"No," Paul responds. "But I will be sure to get up." Tina eases her panties off as the rate of her heart escalates. Paul rolls over on top of Tina as she slightly opens her legs enough for him to rub his penis up and down on the lips of her vagina. He puts himself inside of her. It hurts her a little but as she moistens up she hardly felt a thing. Paul didn't have a big penis and she was thankful for that. He palms her ass cheeks and her legs suddenly spreads wider. Tina rubs her hands up and down his body as she makes facial frowns as her secretions from her pulsating vagina flow down his penis. Shortly after, Paul snatches his penis out of her and skeets off on her little hairy vagina. The next morning Tina woke up with a hangover. Ice Man walks out the room asking, "Are you all ready to go home?"

"Yes!" They all replied. As Sheila relaxes in the bedroom, Ice Man takes Paul and Tina home. Tina walks in on her grandmother standing by the kitchen sink.

"Child where have you been all night long?"

"I slept over at Sheila's house last night Grandma." Tina's Grandma did not care too much for Sheila. Tina goes into her room to find a fresh pair of panties. She heads to the bathroom to shower and from there she falls fast asleep.

Chapter 2

Later that evening Tina receives a call from Sheila. She wanted to know all the details.

"So girl how was your night?"

"Besides getting drunk it was okay," Tina whispers."

"So did you and Paul have sex?"

"Yeah, but it wasn't all that. I don't even know why I gave it up. Now I feel like a whore."

"Girl, you ain't a whore. Things happen. You will forget all about it later. I want you to meet someone. I will call you back around 8 O'clock." Tina finally decides to get up and get dressed. The phone rings, it's Paul.

"How are you doing?"

"I'm fine. Can I call you back later? I'm busy right now."

"Okay," he replied as the phone clicks. About 8:15 Sheila call comes through as promised.

"Hey girl would you like to go to The Maze?"

"Yeah, but we are not old enough to get in that place."

"B-Money is back in town, Ice Man's friend. He knows the manager really good." The Maze was one of the hottest clubs in Charlotte where all the ballas go. The parking lot was filled with big boy cars, exquisite diamonds, platinum and gold and excitement was always promised for a night to remember.

"Sure," Tina said. "If it's like that. Pick me up at 9:00." Ice Man and Sheila pulls up like they were a couple again. He must have fucked her really well last night. She was extra happy to be with him, she thought to herself. When they pull up B-Money was waiting in his 1985 Mercedes Benz. When he got out Tina's mental reaction was, damn he is fine as hell. B-Money was the type of guy who would fuck anybody. He would lay down with a snake if you could hold its head still.

"This is Tina," Ice Man introduced the pair.

"Hi I'm B-money. Y'all follow me." As they enter through the side entrance it seemed as if everybody knew B-Money. He was a regular at The Maze.

"Can I get you ladies a drink?" B-Money inquired.

"Yes! A shot of Hennessey," Sheila said.

"I will have the same," Tina replied.

"Okay ladies follow me to the bar." By then Ice Man eases over to a woman he knew from the streets as the two ladies sip on their drinks. B-Money instructs the bartender to give the ladies whatever they wanted then he walked off. A couple of men approach the ladies at the bar and asked them to dance, so they did. They were having a good time. There were all types of men approaching them.

So they decide to take a seat at a nearby table. Ice Man walks up and grabs Sheila by the hand and asked her, "Can I have this dance?" Leaving Tina alone at the table. After a while B-Money came over to the table where Tina was sitting.

"I heard you just graduated," sparking conversation with Tina.

"Yes, I did," Tina responds with a big smile.

"You have a pretty smile."

"Thank you."

"I saw you out there dropping like it was hot. Now do you want to dance with a real balla?" As they approach the dance floor Tina had no idea that B-Money was a blameless dancer. He danced the socks off of her feet. It was closing time at the club and B-money offered Tina a ride home as Ice Man and Sheila went their way. On the way home B-Money and Tina talked about how they were raised and the old neighborhood they grew up in. They found out they were born and raised on the Northside of Charlotte. They had finally arrived at Tina's house and B-Money reaches and gives Tina a hug.

"Can I get your phone number? Maybe we can hang out sometime."

"Sure." Tina writes down her telephone number and gives it to him.

"Make sure you call me." Tina smiles as she gets out the car. B-Money watches her big round ass walk off until she opens the door and goes in. On the way home B-

Money sees a nice looking lady around 30-years of age walking. She flags him down and asked could she get a ride. It was around 4:30 in the morning. The lady was a crack addict, but she did not look like it. She had long black hair as if she were mixed, with pretty brown skin, small waist and a firm ass.

"So what is a beautiful lady like yourself doing out here this time of morning?"

"My husband and I had an argument and I walked out of the house." She lied. "Now I just want to get high."

"High on what?"

"Crack! Do you know where I can get some?" B-Money starts laughing and said, "Stop playing."

She looks at him and said, "I'm for real. I smoke crack."

"Well I have powder can you cook?"

"Yes, if you have baking soda." She gets in the car and they head towards B-Money's place. When they arrive he gives her what she asked for and she begins to smoke. B-Money lies across his bed with nothing on but his boxers. When she finishes she takes off all her clothes. She was so fine, looked as if she had stepped out of a Playboy magazine. She sat beside him and began to pull out his long black penis. She took her tongue and licks around the head as she slowly thrashes it along the sides of his shaft, stroking her tongue fiercely up and down in a circular motion. At that moment she did something she had never done. She swallowed over half of his penis down her throat. All he could see was her head bobbing up and down. His toes felt like they were going to pop off his feet.

She pulls his boxers completely off and crawls on top easing his penis inside of her wet, juicy vagina. She rode him like he was her rodeo. She bounces up and down on his penis screaming like she was about to cum on him. Then B-Money flips her over on her back and hangs her leg over his shoulder and starts sinking his penis to one side of her vagina, knocking her walls out. Her vagina was so wet. She grabs her ankles and starts rolling her ass. They were both immersed in sweat as she hollers, "Take it out!" As he pulls out she starts to cum. With her legs spread as wide as they could go she begins to shake as she grabs his penis pulling him deeper and deeper back into her. She moans as she tells him how good it feels.

When he busts off inside her, all he could say was, "DAMN!" She had the best vagina he had ever had. Plus, he had never been with an older woman before. They got dressed and she asked him for another bag of powder to go. She wanted to be dropped off close to the Blvd.

She gave him a kiss and said, "I hope we can do this again. Can I have your number?" He gives her his number and said, "Anytime. By the way what is your name?"

"Strawberry," she said, as she opens the car door and hops out. By then the sun was coming up. B-Money was now headed back to his place when a call came through from his pager. It was Lisa, a brod from Southside. When he got in he gave her a call. She wanted an ounce of powder and two ounces of weed.

"I will be there shortly. Give me about thirty minutes." After taking care of business he heads back home. About a week later Tina finds herself a job at a

Kentucky Fried Chicken near her house. She lands her very first job and she was excited about it. She was working as a cashier. Her first day had come and gone and she was a little tired but she liked the fact that she was making her own money. On the way home she runs into Sheila smoking a joint. Sheila had found her a job at McDonald's across the street. They walk together and start talking about the guys. Sheila was telling Tina how happy she was about getting back together with Ice Man. She told her the reason he broke up with her the first time was because he did not like the way she dressed. Sheila liked to wear tight clothes and short skirts. Ice Man was not into that. Now that she has a job she wants to change up her dress code. Plus, Ice Man promised to take her shopping the weekend.

"I really love him," Sheila said, as she passes the joint to Tina. They sit on Tina's front porch. Of course Tina's Grandmother was not at home from work yet.

"You still have not heard from B-Money?"

"No, he must not be interested in me. It's all good because I am not ready for a serious relationship yet."

"Well I will call you later when I get out of the shower," Sheila said.

Then she sees Tina's grandma pull up, "Hey Ms. Mable." Sheila spoke as Ms. Mable opens the car door. Grandma Mable walks up on the porch.

"Hi Grandma." Tina spoke.

"Hi sweetie. How was your first day of work?"

"It was okay," Tina said as they both went inside. Tina showers and helps her grandma prepare dinner. Tina and her grandma were very close. Tina did not know too many of her daddy's people and was not close to her mother's people. With the exception of Grandma Mable. After dinner Tina went into her room and put in her New Edition tape and lays across the bed. The phone rings, she answers and it was B-Money.

"What's up stranger? Sorry I haven't had a chance to call. I have been busy."

"It's cool. I'm glad to hear from you. I thought you had died or something;" She joked.

"So what's up for Saturday night?"

"I don't know, you tell me," Tina said with a smile.

"Would you like to go to dinner and a movie?"

"Sure. You know I started working at the KFC by my house." "Congratulations!"

"Thank you."

"So what time do you get off?"

"4 O'clock."

"I will pick you up tomorrow and give you a ride home... okay?"

"Well I will see you tomorrow." After she completes her conversation with B-Money she decides to call Sheila.

"Girl, B-Money just called me and he is taking me to dinner and a movie Saturday. He said he was going to pick me up from work tomorrow." When they finished talking Tina got ready for bed. The next day after work B-Money was waiting on Tina when she got off work. She walks to the car with a smile on her face.

"How are you doing?"

"Good, now that I've seen you again." B-Money responded. They pull off and head in a different direction from where Tina lives.

"Where are we going?" Tina inquired.

"To the mall." He had a surprise for Tina. She sat quietly as the sounds of Run DMC came from the speakers. When they arrive at the mall B-Money tells her to find herself a nice short set and a pair of Air Jordan's. If that was what she wanted. And that is what she did.

She told him, "You didn't have to. That's why I have a job."

"I know. But I can't help wanting to spend money on someone as pretty as yourself. Besides I want to get to know you better."

"You don't have to spend money on me to get to know me better. You don't have to spend money to do that." Tina simplified.

"Well it's too late now," as they walk the mall. Afterwards B-Money drops Tina off at home.

"I will call you tomorrow. When she got out the car he watches her ass swing from left to right on that beautiful Thursday evening.

CHAPTER 3

Saturday had finally come and Tina was anxious to get off of work. The clock strikes 4 PM and she heads for the door. As usual Sheila was standing on the sidewalk waiting with a joint between her fingers. The two start walking towards the house and Sheila alerts Tina that she would call her later. Tina heads in and greets her grandmother with a kiss. Tina fast forward towards the bathroom to shower and notices that her period had come on. Oops. You won't be getting none tonight, she laughs to herself. She showers, teases her ponytail and puts on her new clothes that B-money had purchased for her at the mall. She applies a little makeup and admires how beautiful she is in the mirror with her new kicks and outfit. About an hour later B-Money calls.

"Are you ready?"

"Yes," Tina replied.

"I'm on my way." B-Money shows up about twenty minutes later. As they drive off they talk a little and laugh a lot like they had known one another for years. He took Tina to Red Lobster because it was his favorite restaurant. He loves seafood.

"Don't be shy. Order anything you want," B-Money expressed.

"Don't worry." Tina said. They both ordered steak and lobster and had a few mixed drinks. It was twenty minutes after seven and the movie started in twenty-five minutes. So they had no other choice but to take off. Once inside the theater B-Money grabs Tina by her hand and kisses her on the cheek. They sit close to the front, in the middle of the theater. After the movie ends, B-Money and Tina head back towards his place. They sit in the living room and watch the news and made great conversation with each other. Then B-money turns the lights down low and shuts the TV off.

They started kissing as she pushes him back saying, "I can't."

"What's wrong?" He asked.

"I'm on my period. And besides we need to take things slow. I like you a lot and you're a great guy but give me some time to get to know you better."

"That's cool. I can wait." They kiss again, even though her vagina was getting hot and wet. She knew she was doing the right thing. They end up having more conversation for about an hour before he took her home.

"Thank you," she said as she leans towards him planting a juicy kiss on his lips. "Call me tomorrow." Tina added. B-Money hated that because he was hornier than a motherfucker. It was past 12 AM so he decides to ride through the Blvd. He runs into Strawberry just standing on the corner. He pulls over and let the window down.

"What happened, you and your husband get into another fight?" She smiles and hops in. As they ride off,

Strawberry could not stop feeling on B-Money's penis. And he could not wait to get her back in his bed. Strawberry made the fourth woman this week he had slept with. However, he knew this would be the best. When they got to the house, Strawberry asked for a drink. B-Money gave her a bag of powder to cook up and poured her a glass of Hennessey. After a few hits and drinks he charms her into his bedroom. He gets naked as she smokes her last bit of crack. She takes her clothes off and starts sucking his penis, slowly putting it down her throat without the need to gasp for air. Strawberry straddles him, rolling around on top of him screaming and licking as she fondles her nipples to an erect state. Strawberry got up and stood by the edge of the bed.

"Come stand behind me. I have something special for you," Strawberry said seductively, as she takes her fingers and rubs her vagina juices in her asshole. She grabs him by his penis slowly as she eases it inside of her ass, she moans. All of a sudden he was up in her deep and the only thing he could think was she was too good to be true. No other woman had ever given him this type of treatment that Strawberry was giving him. She pushes him back and lay flat on her back, separating her vagina lips as she spreads her legs apart. Strawberry was a real freak and an undercover prostitute, who had been in the streets for six months. B-Money straddles her and grabs her butt cheeks pulling her softly towards him. He was going deep and hard inside of her pulsating vagina, just the way she liked it. She was screaming like he was killing her, taking all eleven inches of his shaft inside of her. Then she whispers, "Slow down and make love to me." When he slows down she rolls slowly in rhythm with his low-toned moans. It was feeling really good to the both of them. Sweat was pouring off of their bodies as his big penis throbs deep inside of her, touching the bottom of her world as her eyes roll in the back of her head, while his tongue swishes around inside of her mouth. They began to kiss slowly and from out of nowhere he whispers, "I don't want you to leave tonight. When we finish I just want to hold you." Strawberry busts a nut and pushes him up off of her. Slowly going down his chest towards his penis to suck it some more. She jacks his penis until he cums in her mouth. After their sexual escapade they get up and shower together. Once out of the shower B-Money gave Strawberry another bag of powder to cook up. He went in the back room and took him a snort. While Strawberry was smoking, B-Money fixes them a drink. They indulge in more conversation and when they finished they went back sexing again.

"Oh Baby, I think I'm in love," Strawberry whispers, as she wraps her legs around his waist. She hugs him real tight like she didn't want to ever let him go. The next morning when they woke up he notices an alert on his pager; 213-7068 was the number that came through. He rushes to the phone and punches in the numbers.

"What's up homie? I need four birds." This is the code for needing four-ounces of powder.

"I'll be there in a few." He tells Strawberry to chill and that he would be right back. When B-Money left Strawberry got up out of the bed. She walks around the house taken notice of all the nice things B-Money has. She goes out back on the patio and thinks to herself what it would be like to get off the street and live like B-Money. After a while she went back in and climbs back in the bed to watch TV. Before she knew it she had fell asleep again. It was around 9:00 AM when he arrives at Chilly's. When he got in Chilly's cousin Sabrina was getting out of the shower. She was also one of B-Money's exes. Sabrina was still in love with B-Money, but she could not put up with his lying and cheating ways. However, they remained friends. After B-Money and Chilly handled business, Sabrina calls B-Money to her room. When he reaches the threshold she was sitting on the bed with a gown on showing off her legs. Her luscious thighs had a tattoo of a rose with letters Slim Goody written under it.

"So whatcha been up to?" Sabrina asked.

"Nothing much but chilling." They talked for about thirty minutes and then he left. When he returns home Strawberry was still asleep. So he quietly got her clothes and shoe sizes. He wanted to surprise her so he took off and went to the mall to do some shopping. He bought her different styles of clothes. From shorts, dresses, to sexy skirts and stylish shoes to compliment her new outfits. After shopping he stops by a nearby restaurant and picks up something for the both of them to eat. When he arrives back to the house, Strawberry was laying across the bed naked.

"Hi sexy, I bought you something to wear. I would like for you to stay with me for a few days." That's all she needed to hear. She felt as if God had answered her prayers.

"I would also like for you to chill on the dope. I like you a lot and you are too beautiful to be killing yourself," he added.

She rises up and gives him a hug and replied, "Thank you."

"Here is something to eat. Here's new underwear and a toothbrush in one of those bags over there." After eating they both shower and spent a quiet relaxing evening alone. They watched TV and had a few drinks. B-Money was falling in love with Strawberry. And she was honored because she was tired of the streets. Two days later B-Money gives Tina a call. She had just finished eating dinner with her grandma.

"Hi Tina," he said, as if he was feeling guilty for not keeping in touch.

"Hey B-Money." She replied. "Would you like to go

for a ride? I won't keep you out late. I know you have to go to work tomorrow."

"Sure." She said. Tina readies herself for her ride out with B-Money and when he arrives she was waiting on the front porch. When she got in the car he gives her a big hug and a kiss. He takes her to a nearby park. They talk for about an hour and he drops her back off at home. Mrs. Mable was not feeling very well so she asked Tina to go to the store for some Pepto Bismol. On her way to the store she bumps into Brian, her ex-boyfriend from high school.

"Hi Tina." Said Brian. "So whatcha been up to these days?" He added.

"Nothing but working." Tina voiced.

"Yeah, I heard you work at KFC."

"Yes I do."

"Maybe I will stop through sometime just to talk to you."

"That will be cool." They were still friends even though Brian always wanted more than Tina wanted to give. He could not wait for that. So they walk off. Tina returns home, checks on her Grandma and goes into her room. She relaxes on her bed and picks up a magazine she had bought with New Edition on the front cover. She heard that they were coming to the Charlotte Coliseum and she wanted to be there. She was the groups biggest fan. She picks up the phone and calls Sheila.

"Girl you know New Edition is coming to Charlotte in two weeks."

"I know and we need to be there."

"No doubt. Guess who else is coming with them?" Tina asked.

"Ready for the World and Salt & Pepa"

"Hell yeah we gotta go."

"So should we double date or take ourselves?" Tina asked.

"I don't know. I will talk to B-Money and Ice Man and see what they say and I will let you know." Said Shelia.

"I will talk to you tomorrow." Tina and Sheila hang up. Two weeks later Tina and Sheila ends up going to the show by themselves. And they kind of enjoyed it better that way. Ready for the World opened up, doing all right by the ladies' standards. Salt and Pepa came on stage and did their thing of course and when New Edition came out the crowd went crazy. Sheila and Tina were jumping and screaming like fresh graduates out of high school. After the show they walked across the street to the Waffle House to use the phone to call Sheila's mom. A couple of guys were hitting on them while they waited for her to pick them up. Tina gave the guy a fake name and number, she really did not want to be bothered in the first place. About 30 minutes later Sheila's mom pulls up and they went home. When Shelia got in she gave Tina a call. They talked about the show and how they would love to fuck the entire group of New Edition. Ralph Tresvant was Tina's favorite out of the group. She even had a few pictures of Prince and Michael Jackson on her wall. After talking for over an hour they decided it was time for them to both hang up and go to bed.

CHAPTER 4

Two months had passed and Strawberry had moved in with B-Money. And she was really enjoying herself. He had her spoiled. Even though he was still kicking it with Tina, he still had not gotten her vagina yet. Tina had a birthday coming up. She was turning 19. B-Money had made plans to take her to the club and during the same week, Sheila and Ice Man had broken up again. She was hurt after catching him kissing another woman in front of the store. He denies it and of course Sheila was not buying it, because she knew what she saw. Sheila lived with her mother, brother and sister. She was the oldest. Her mother had a good job at Lance Potato Chip Company and had been there for sixteen years. As the days' passed, the week of Tina's birthday was finally here. Her birthday was on a Wednesday. B-Money picked her up and took her home. He surprised her with a big diamond ring. She kisses him all over after he parks in front of the house. A few minutes later Grandma Mable drives up, as Tina hops out of the car.

She says to Tina, "I hope you are not having sex young lady." Not knowing that it was too late for that speech. Mrs. Mable was real old-fashioned. She didn't believe in shacking up or sex before marriage.

"No Grandma, He is just a friend." Tina lied.

"Hmmm," Grandma Mable mumbles as she unlocks the door and goes inside. Tina sits on the porch, waiting for Sheila to come through. A few minutes later she pops up.

"Hey girl." Tina just smiles and sticks her hand out.

"Damn," Sheila hollers as her eyes gets big.

"It's a birthday present from B-Money."

"Girl you know you have to break him off."

"I know," Tina said, still smiling.

"Well I brought a joint with me for your birthday."

"In that case damn near every day is my birthday," the two laughed. Then Tina got high. She really smiles a lot and Sheila was cracking jokes.

"Well girl it's about time for me to roll out." So Tina walks Sheila halfway home. She only stayed around the corner. They talk about Ice-Man. Sheila was telling Tina how she loves and misses him. When Tina got back to the house B-Money calls. He just wanted to talk. The following Saturday, B-Money scoops Tina up to go to the club for her birthday. He told Strawberry he would not be back tonight because he had to go out of town to pick up some dope. But he left her with two bags of powder and a fifth of Hennessey.

When they enter the club he told her, "I hope you are ready to party." Tina was really feeling him. Especially for the things he had done for her.

"Yes, I'm ready to party."

"Good." He ordered two shots of Hennessey and they chill at the table while they drank. Then he orders some chicken wings and potato wedges. And they dance. Afterwards, he puts in another order of shots. Before the night was over they both had consumed five shots a piece. Tina was feeling good. B-Money held on to her as they made their way to the car. They left the club around 1:30 AM and arrive at the Marriott Hotel.

She asked, "Why are we here? Why can't we go to your house?"

"No! My two cousins are here from out of town. I want to be alone with you." B-Money registers a room for the both of them. When they get to the room he turns on the lamp.

"Make yourself comfortable and I will be right out." He went in the bathroom and took two snorts up the nose. When he came out Tina had already taken off her clothes. She knew what time it was. She was already under the covers with her eyes close. B-Money sits on the edge of the bed to check his pager and then he takes off all his clothes. The room was nice and cool from the air conditioner. B-Money reaches over to kiss her on the lips. As he kisses her she spreads her legs apart and starts rubbing on her hairy vagina. He stimulates her clit and massages his way down to sticking his moist finger in her vagina. He softly kisses her on her neck. Tina was getting horny. B-Money didn't pull any punches as he sucks on her pretty little titties, she got even wetter. She was high and horny, as she winds fast on B-Money's fingers. B-Money goes down between her legs and eats her vagina.

She smells so fresh and clean, as if she had douched with roses. When he came up for air he sticks the head of his penis inside of her and moans in satisfaction. Tina's vagina was tight. Brain nor Paul were near the same size as B-Money. Plus, B-Money had plenty of experience when it came to sex. He took his hand and forces his penis in slowly as her eyes roll in the back of her head. She starts crying about two minutes later. Tears were slowly running down her face. She was about to put her nails into his skin. B-Money told her to ball her fist up she would not scratch him. He knew she had to be damn near a virgin as tight as she was. But he was going to make sure she remembered this night. He grabs her by her right ankle and holds it up in the air. Then he lays her leg across his shoulder as he plunges the left side of her vagina.

"Oh please take it easy!" She screams silently. B-Money put both of her legs on his shoulders and went deep, as she cried even more. Her wet vagina was popping and smacking, making conversation with B-Money. He is turned on by the noises coming from between her legs. About fifteen minutes later Tina had nutted so hard she stuck her nails in his arms. She let out a scream and cried, as her tight vagina got wetter. It felt so good to B-Money but Tina was in a lot of pain. Her stomach was hurting and it felt as if he was punching her bladder. She was afraid to ask him to get up.

She cried, "Oh God please," over and over again, which sounded really good to B-Money. He turned her around and stuck it in from the back. She started screaming because he spread her ass cheeks apart while he beat her vagina real hard. Tina bawls and screeches as she buries her face in the pillow. He continues beating it harder and harder, faster and faster. He knew he had bust Tina wide open. She was even wetter and her vagina walls were loosening up. When he looks down, he notices as he's going in and out of her that blood was on his penis. He was about to cum inside of her. He didn't say a thing. He told her to lay on her back. They had been fucking for two hours now and she was in pain.

He told Tina, "Fuck me back," because he was about to cum. Tina looked away with tears in her pretty little eyes and said, "I will try."

She was breathing hard and so was B-Money. When he eases it in it wasn't as tight because of her cum and the blood. Tina had no idea she was bleeding. He begins rolling slow and she grabs him tight and winds back, matching his rhythm. Then her legs flew open as she bust another nut. Her wet vagina starts popping and smacking again as B-Money went deep and hard, hitting corners and all. Then he finally came inside of her. He lays on top of her letting all of his cum run inside of her.

He kisses her saying, "I love you."

Tina softly replies, "I love you too."

Then B-Money got up and said, "I think you better go check yourself." She pulls the covers back and notices the blood on the sheets. She jumps up and grab her panties and go to the bathroom. She sits on the toilet in pain. Her stomach was hurting and so was her vagina. About five minutes later she got a rag and washes herself up. Then she pads her panties with tissue. When she came out she asked B-Money if he would take her home.

"Are you okay?" B-Money asked.

"Yes, I am. But I need to go home." B-Money goes in the bathroom to wash up and get dressed to take Tina home. On the way out the door he gives her a hug and a kiss on the forehead.

"I'm sorry," he says.

"It's okay. I am a big girl."

"I can't tell," with a smile on his face joking. They both laugh and she hits him on his arm. They leave the room around 4:15 AM to drop her off. As she was getting out of the car he grasps her by the hand and said, "I really do love you." She stares and kisses him and then gets out of the car. He watches her walking funny all the way to the door. When B-Money finally arrives home he realizes that Strawberry was still awake. Not knowing she had just come in five minutes before he did. She had been out on the Blvd turning tricks. Now she was nervous and hoping he did not want any sex out of her because her panties were still wet with cum from two other men she had fucked earlier. He kisses her and hops in the shower. As he is doing that Strawberry was doing the same. She was so scared she washed up in the kitchen sink. She wraps her panties up in newspaper and threw it away in the trash outdoors. Then she went and jumps in the bed naked pretending to be tired. B-Money gets out the shower and lay beside Strawberry and give her a hug and a kiss, and then they both fell asleep. The next morning B-Money decides he wants to sell crack, powder and weed. So he calls around for connections. He gets in touch with an old friend by the name of CJ. He was bigger in the game than B-Money. He owned a mansion on the lake in ATL. They talk short and smooth and set up to meet the next day. So B-Money took a drive to the ATL the next morning. He invested in two keys of crack to start off with and heads back to Charlotte. When he arrives he called Ice Man first and then he reaches out to the rest of his workers. He asked them if they were interested in selling crack. All of them were down for it. He told them he would hit them off tomorrow. B-Money spent the entire night weighing and bagging up dope. He gave Strawberry about a gram to test. He knew the dope was good because she just sat on the couch shell without a peep coming out of her. He liked the way she handled hers. She was not like most crack addicts. Picking off the floor, peeking out the window and talking about be quiet the police are outside. About 10 minutes later she goes to pour them a drink and kisses him on the cheek as she sits back down on the couch.

Chapter 5

It was a nice Sunday afternoon, Ice Man had just gotten off the phone with B-Money and then Sheila calls.

"We need to talk." She said.

"Yes. I am on my way." He replied. When he picked her up she was looking real sexy. Her hair looked as if she had just left out of the salon. They went to the park and sat at a picnic table and watched a game of softball. She looks at him and says, "I love you." And then she sticks her tongue in his mouth. After she kisses him she slaps him on the side of his head.

"You are going to have to stop treating me like shit."

"I'm sorry he said. I made a mistake. I know we can make this relationship work."

As he reaches out to hug her, "I don't know what I will do without you. You are a very special lady to me. You are always there for me and I love you for that."

"Then why do you continue to play games if you love me the way you say you do?" She asked.

"I don't know," he honestly replied. "But I am going to change because don't want to lose you."

"Well you are not going to get my pants off until you prove to me you really love me." They got up and took a walk around the nature trail and came back and watched some more of the softball game. After the game he took her out to eat at Prime Ribs. While sitting at the table Sheila asked Ice Man to buy her a ring. She never asked him for much and of course he said yes.

"We can go get it tomorrow." They talked and enjoyed the food. Ice Man was crazy about the ribs. The next day he picked her up from work and took her Friedman's Jewelers. She picked out a beautiful ring with diamonds all in it. She loved the way it shined. It wasn't as nice as Tina's but she didn't want Ice Man to spend a lot of money on the ring. He looks at her and smiles. Then he springs the big question, "Would you like to get an apartment together?" Sheila did not know what to say.

"Let me talk to my mother first and I will get back to you." She knew her mother was not going to like the idea of her moving out, but she had already made up her mind to do so. When she got home she told her mother she would be moving out soon. Her mother did not put up an argument. Sheila went into her room and called Tina.

Tina answered, "What's up girl?"

"Nothing just got through eating. I got Ice Man to buy me a ring today. You know I was jealous."

"Girl that's what's up," Tina said.

"It's not as nice as yours but it's pretty."

"It's the thought that counts. So are you and Ice Man back together for the hundredth time?"

"Yes, and we are moving in together as soon as we find a place. So, did you break B-Money off?

"Yes, I gave him a lil bit."

"How was it girl?"

"He was good." Tina didn't want to tell all of her details about how he busts her and made her bleed. After they got off the phone Tina start counting up the money she had been saving. She always put something back from her check. Plus, B-Money gives her money. She was ready to take the driving test and buy a car. So far she had saved up $943.00 and she gets paid tomorrow to add more to it. She gets paid every Monday from her job. She went in the living room to talk with Grandma Mable. She asked her if she could work a half a day on Friday so she can take the driving test. She had already studied the book and successfully passed the driver's education class. Grandma Mable agreed. When Friday rolled around, Tina had the day off so Grandma Mable could take her to handle business at the DMV. Tina was the fourth person in line. She had her book and she continued studying until it was her turn. When her name was called to take the test she felt a little nervous. But she passed with flying colors and drove well on the streets during the driving test. When she arrived back to take her picture for her license she blew a kiss at her Grandma. Afterwards, her Grandma drops her back off at the house and she went on to work. Tina took a cab to the Honda dealership not far from where she lived. She walks around looking at all the nice cars on the lot. Then she spots a 1981 Honda Accord for $3300. She really wanted it and she knew just how she was going to get it.

She went to the street to use the pay phone and paged B-Money. He called her back about five minutes later. She told him she needed a ride home. When he picked her up he inquired to what she was doing at the gas station. So she told him about her getting her license and looking at some cars.

"That's good," he said. "Now you can start driving me around." She didn't tell him about the car she wanted. She was going to wait until she fucked him again. When they reached her house, she invited him in for a minute. She takes him to her room and he lounges on her bed as he jokes with her about Michael Jackson. He really teased her.

"Mike is gay as hell."

"Don't talk about Mike like that. He kissed Tina and laid her flat on the bed. He touches her vagina, as she screeches, "Not right now my grandma will be home in a few."

"Well can I see you tonight then?"

"Yes." She said. She walks him to the door and tells him, "I love you."

"I love you too sexy!" When B-Money left he hooks up with Ice Man. He tells him about his adventures he had been having with Tina and Strawberry, while they ride around smoking a joint and laughing. Now Ice Man had something he wanted to tell B-Money.

"Hey man we been cool and all, but I think I'm ready to start working for myself."

"That's cool lil bruh. You'll be buying weight from me."

"No doubt. Who else?" Then they shook hands. They dropped off a package to Rick, one of B-Money's workers. He was only 28-years old driving an 84 Cadillac and had been in the game with B-Money for years. They are good friends. Rick could sell four to five ounces in a week. His spot was always jumping. Rick began telling Ice and B how he and Corey drugged some girl a week ago. Corey was another one of B-Money's workers. He said she was so fine and a straight freak. He never fully described her because if he did; B-Money would have known he was talking about Strawberry. Then Rick fired up a joint with his favorite lighter, the kind you put fluid in when it ran out. He had that lighter ever since he first started selling dope. He called it his lucky lighter because he had never been to jail. After they left B-money drops Ice Man off. Then Sheila calls to let Ice Man know that she had found a 2-bedroom apartment for $425 a month. They went to look at it and found it was nice so they gave the rent man a call. B-Money went home and chilled with Strawberry. She had dinner ready and the house was clean. She greeted him at the door with a kiss. He knew what she wanted so he gave her a gram to keep her satisfied because he knew she was suspect; she was a prostitute before he met her. About three hours later he told her to dress up nice he was going to take her to the club. Then he called Tina and told her he would see her later around 12. He told her he had to take care of some business. She told him she would be waiting for his call. When B-Money got to the club he introduced Strawberry to a couple of people. Then they ran into Rick.

He introduces them as they look at one another. She knew exactly who Rick was and he could not forget a face like hers. Especially the way she threw that vagina on him. They had a few drinks on Rick and did some dancing. B-Money gave Strawberry a $50 bill and told her to enjoy herself. He had to make a run and would be back shortly. It was 11:45 and he calls Tina from a pay phone to let her know he was on his way. When he pulls up at Tina's house she comes out with a short skirt on. She was looking real sexy as usual. She gets in the car and kisses him. When they arrive he informs her that he has to be somewhere in two hours. He took her to the guest bedroom so she would not see Strawberry belongings. When he laid her on the bed she asked him not to fuck her hard. He pulled her skirt and panties off and then took off his clothes. He kisses and rubs on Tina's vagina and stick his fingers inside of her to get it wet. He slowly eases his penis inside of her, trying hard not to hurt her. He rolls slowly putting more of him inside of her until he reaches the bottom. She started moan but all she could think about was that Honda she wanted and she prepared herself to fuck him back no matter how much it hurt.

He got his entire shaft inside of her tight vagina and spreads her legs wide as she cries out, "Oh Baby! I love you. Oh Baby! I love you." She was rolling back even though it hurt like hell as he went deeper and with ease. He began to lick her ears and suck on her nipples. He had been in her for about thirty minutes. Tina was horny, real horny. She busts a nut but B-Money just roll nice and slow and easy in that vagina. He gets up and puts Tina on top of him. It was her first time riding a penis. When he slid his penis inside of her, she moves around real fast and screams. He holds her by her small waist as he lifts his body off the bed grinding in her, beating the vagina up. She jumps off crying, "Baby take it easy. You are going to make me bleed again." So he rolls over on top of her and bust a nut about twenty minutes later. He lays between her legs and let his cum run inside of her.

"Thank you." She said.

"For what?" He replied.

"For not fucking me real hard like the last time."

"You are my girl and I want you to get use to this penis. I love you and I want to satisfy you in every way possible." She knew she had him where she wanted him but she was not going to mention the car just yet, she wanted to wait a little while longer. They take a shower and he hit it again from the back in the shower. At the same time, he was thinking about Strawberry. When he got out of the shower he went into the living room and paged himself. He hears his pager go off in the room and he goes in to check it.

"Damn baby. I told you I had to be somewhere. Let's get dressed so I can drop you off." On his way to take Tina home she was not looking very happy. She was quiet as a church mouse. He looked over at her and held her hand.

"Are you okay beautiful?"

"No, not really."

"Then what's the matter?"

"I thought maybe I would be able to chill with my man tonight."

"Baby you know that shit can get dangerous sometimes. I cannot get you caught up." When he got her home he kisses her and says her he loves her.

Chapter 6

Back at the club, Strawberry had been getting her drink on and Rick was putting his game down. He was really disrespecting B-Money behind his back. He asked Strawberry when could he see her again as he slips her a gram of crack. She puts it in her pocket and tells him soon. He gives her his number and tells her to call him and walks off. B-Money gets back to the club at closing time.

"You ready to go sweetheart?" He grabs her by the hand and leads her to the door. "Baby I missed you," he says to Strawberry. "I have been ready to go home," he added. Rick had no idea that Strawberry was living with B-Money. When they got home they both got naked and jumped in the bed. They continued telling one another how much they love each other. B-Money still had enough energy to break her off. That Sunday morning, they got dressed to go to the mall in Pineville. He did not want to be seen with her too much in Charlotte. He was afraid that Tina would catch him. He really loved Tina but he was also smitten by Strawberry and she knew it. There was nothing B-Money would not do for her. Even kill! As they walk around the mall holding hands B-Money bought her whatever she wanted. He even got her some jewelry and afterwards they stop by an ice cream parlor to eat. When they got done with shopping they head back to the house and then B-Money receives a page from Tina.

He calls her and inquired, "What's up baby?"

"Nothing," she responded. I just want to see you."

"About 7." After Tina hangs up the phone there was a knock on the door. It was Sheila. Sheila fires up a joint as they sit on the porch. After they smoked the joint they decided to go for a short walk. A guy in a red Camaro stops them to see if they needed a ride.

"No we're fine," they holler. As he drives off Tina was thinking about the Honda and how it was about time for her to ask B-Money to handle that for her. Sheila was telling her about their new apartment and how well she and Ice Man were getting along. Tina had to return home because it was soon time for B-Money to arrive. Sheila figured she would go see her mother for a while. At 6:45 B-Money pulls up. Tina opens the door and gets in the car. They went to the movies and then got a late night snack before he dropped her back off at home. She looked at him as if she was not getting out the car.

"What's wrong baby? I'm turning in early tonight." He said.

"So what are you saying, I can't go home with you?"

"No because I need some rest. I am tired baby."

"And what is wrong with me resting beside you? Tina asked.

"Please Tina, not tonight." Tina jumps out the car mad. She was also hurt that B-Money did not want to be bothered with her. She went inside and lay across her bed as she begins to feel sorry for slamming B-Money's car door. About 30 minutes later she gives him a page. Strawberry was in the bedroom watching TV so he walks in the kitchen to give her a call. When she answers she tells him she was sorry for slamming his car door.

"That's alright." He said.

"I just love being with you but you are always busy."

"Well baby you know how I make my living."

"I know but I would like to see you a little more often."

"Baby girl I will do my best to make that happen for you." That made Tina feel really good. Now it was time for her to pop the question.

"Can you help me buy a car?"

"What kind of car?"

"I saw a 1981 Honda Accord I want."

"How much is it?"

"$3300.00." She said.

"No problem. We can go look at it on Monday." They talked about some other things before he told her goodnight. When Monday came around B-Money picked Tina up from work. Tina was excited. When they arrive at the car lot she shows B-Money the car. They walk around the car checking it out. Then B-Money walked three cars down. It was a black 84 model sitting there so he asked her if she liked it.

She replied, "Yes, but of course it cost too much."

"I didn't ask you how much it cost. I asked if you like the car."

"She smiles and said, "Yes." B-Money found a salesman to come over with the keys so that Tina could take a test drive. When she got back they went in and took care of the paperwork. Then B-Money followed Tina home so she could park her car and jump in with him. They rode around for a few hours talking about this and that before he dropped her off at home. She called Sheila and told her the good news and when she got off the phone with Sheila she told Grandma Mable to look out the door.

She asked Tina, "Whose car is that?"

"That's my car grandma."

"How can you afford a car like that? She told her that she had been saving up her money but she still owed a little bit more on it. She didn't tell her grandma that B-Money had paid for it. By this time the excitement of her day had made her tired. So it was time to shower and go to sleep. The next morning Tina picked Sheila up and dropped her off at work. Then she went to work. When they both got off they went riding around the city. When they stopped for gas they ran into Paul riding in an 85 Cutlass. He had found him a job at FED-X.

"What's up ladies?" He said.

"Nothing much." They replied. Paul walked around to Tina.

"Why haven't you called me?" She told him she had a boyfriend and that she was sorry that she had not called him.

"That's cool. You know I'm getting married next month?"

"Well good for you," as Tina walks around to pump her gas, Sheila comes out of the store. "Well take care of yourself Paul and congratulations on your engagement." They stop by the music store so Tina could get the latest LL Cool J tape.

Chapter 7

It was the year 1989 and nothing much had changed. April was coming in and it felt as if it was going to be another hot summer. B-Money was still doing his thing and Ice Man had blown up also. Sheila was no longer working at McDonalds. She was now helping Ice Man with his business. She knew every connect and who smoked. She knew how to weigh, bag and sell dope. Tina was going to beauty school on Beatties Ford Road. B-Money ended up paying her way. Strawberry was still living with B-Money, but she was sneaking around with Rick every chance she got when B was in Atlanta. Tina had invited B-Money to come to church with her and Grandma Mable for Easter. Afterwards, they ate dinner. Later that night B-Money took Strawberry to the club. They had a good time. Even though Rick was there. He was smiling and joking with B-Money like everything was all right. He even asked B-Money if he could dance with Strawberry. B-Money said yes. He didn't think nothing of it. Later that morning, he took Strawberry home and fucked her really well. Even though she loved B-Money she was also feeling Rick. On July 2, B-Money rode to Atlanta and took Tina with him. He had to pick up some dope and really did not want to take her, but she insisted on going. Later that morning, on the way back he spots Strawberry hoping in a car with Rick. He could not believe his eyes.

"Ain't that a bitch," he mumbles under his breath.

"What's wrong?" Tina asked.

"Nothing!" All this time he was thinking he was getting played. He drops Tina off at home and goes home. He parks his car around back, goes inside and sits on the couch. He was mad as hell. Meanwhile, Rick had Strawberry at his brother's house. Every time she got with Rick he would give her an eight ball and she would suck and fuck him anyway he liked. He had fucked her for about an hour. As soon as he bust inside of her his brother came through the door. They got in an argument over some money. So Rick and Strawberry put on their clothes and left. Back at the house, B-Money was getting madder by the second. He took a couple of shots of Hennessey and a few snorts of powder. Then he starts thinking about how he met Strawberry and all of the freaky kinky stuff she had done to him. Around 6:15 in the morning, he gets ready for bed and he hears something coming from the front of the house. It was Strawberry. When she saw him she got scared as hell, because when he left for Atlanta he was happy. For some reason she knew she was in for it.

"Where the hell have you been?"

"Over a girlfriend's house."

"Oh yeah! Pull off your panties?"

"For what?"

"Take them off I said!"

"No!"

"What the hell is wrong with you?" (SMACK) She falls to the floor.

"Please I will take them off. Just don't hit me." Her vagina was still running with her and Rick's cum. She gave him the panties with fear in her eyes. He could feel and see the stains in her panties. He beats her with his fist. She was bleeding from her nose. Then he pulls out his .357 and puts it to her head.

"Bitch I'm going to ask you one more time and one more time only and if you lie to me I'm going to kill you. So who did you fuck?" As she trembles in fear, tears roll down her face. She had never seen B-Money like this before. She finally admits, it was Rick, as she grabs his leg and begs him not to kill her.

"I'm sorry baby. Please don't kill me," she kept saying over and over again.

"I love you! Please give me another chance." As much as he hates her at this moment he pulls her up and tells her to get in the shower. While she was in the shower he draws a couple of snorts in and a few drinks. He felt he needed to get high and drunk to come down off of his emotions. He gets in the bed. She later came in crying a little as she lays beside him.

"Baby please forgive me. It only happened a few times. I get lonely sometimes when you would be away."

"Well bitch, I will get you a dildo to keep you company while I am gone." Then he takes his penis out and shoves her head down. She was sucking as he was trying to choke the life out of her. He lays her on her back and puts her legs on his shoulders. He stood up in her vagina, dropping down as hard as he could for twenty minutes. It was nothing she could do but scream. He went deep as he could, hitting everything that was in the way. He then turns her around and sticks his penis in her ass. He was hitting her so hard it was popping. Tears were running down her face as she begs him to stop. He was trying to punish her. He was fucking her so hard she springs off his penis and hits her head against the headboard. He pulls her back towards him and sticks his penis back inside of her as she cries even more. He fucks her in her ass for at least 40 minutes until he came inside of her. When he finished, she went to the bathroom to wipe off and then came back to wipe him down clean. As she lays back down she tells him, "I still love you B-Money no matter how much you punish me." She tries to kiss him but he turns away. The next morning when he gets up Strawberry was gone. He didn't know what to think. She returns with some groceries. She had taken the car and went to the store. She didn't say a thing. She washes her hands and fix breakfast. B-Money was thinking, maybe she does love me as he turns on the TV. She brought him his plate of food in the room and left back out. When he finished eating he went to the kitchen to put his plate in the sink. He sits on the couch next to her, gives her a hug and tells her, "I am sorry." She kisses him and said, "It's okay. I was wrong for what I did." They cuddle up with one another and watch a movie. Then Tina pulls up. He hears her car door slam. He goes to the door and walks outside closing it behind him. He doesn't say a word. He grabs her arm and leads her back to the car.

"Didn't I tell you not to be popping up over here? Call before you come."

"I'm sorry I just wanted to make sure you were alright. You looked upset when you dropped me off this morning."

"I'm fine now. It's not a good time for you to be here. I got some people on the way with a lot of dope."

"So you're not dealing with CJ no more?"

"Tina just leave. I will call you later and in the near future you call before you pop up." Tina was not feeling that. She felt B-Money was hiding something, but she got in her car and left. While B-Money was talking to Tina, Strawberry was peeping out of the window. When he came back inside, she asked no questions. He told her Tina was looking for some weed. Later that evening, Tina pages B-Money but he didn't return her call. He just wanted to chill with Strawberry. After Sunday morning breakfast with Grandma Mable, a shower and getting dressed, Tina decides to give Sheila a call. She asked her if she wanted to go out for a ride. They rode to the mall and purchased a few things and then went to North Charlotte. She remembered her dad having a sister that lived on Fleetwood Ave. She had not seen her since she was a little girl, but she remembers where she lives because her grandma had passed by there and pointed it out a few times. When they pull up there was a lady in the yard watering the grass. Tina and Sheila get out and walk towards the lady.

"Aunt Alice," Tina said.

The woman looks and said, "Tina is that you?"

"Yes, it's me."

"Girl look at you. You're all grown up. Come give your Aunt a hug." Tina introduces her Aunt and Sheila and they relaxed under a shade tree to catch up. They talk for hours. Tina let her Aunt know she had to go and her Aunt let her know to not be a stranger and to come back to see her. Tina agreed. They stop for ice cream but Tina also wanted to ride by B-Money's house. Then she thought if he sees her he would be mad at her for spying. So she opted not to and takes Sheila home. When she got in Ice Man greets her with a kiss.

"Did you enjoy your morning out?"

"Yes," she said. When Tina got home she gave B-Money a page. He calls her back. They talk for a good while. When she gets off the phone with him she took out her new clothes because tomorrow was the 4th of July. It was a steamy hot summer day and everyone was cooking out. Tina spent the holiday with Sheila and her family and would catch up with the guys later. A lot of Sheila's family came over, including Sheila's cousin Bug who was sweating Tina. The music was playing and the kids were popping firecrackers and there was a lot of drinking and eating going on. It looked more like a family reunion. Later that day B-Money and Ice Man hooks up. He told him how Rick had stabbed him in the back. How he had been fucking Strawberry and now it was time for him to pay. Ice Man was down because he never really liked Rick no way. Ever since Rick hit him in the head back in the day. B-Money gives Rick a call and asked him to meet him behind the old school on Lakeside by 10 o'clock. He tells him that he had a deal going down that involved a lot of money and drugs. Rick didn't think nothing of it. He agrees to meet B-Money. About 9:45 B-Money pulls up behind the apartments. It was dark and there were neighborhood kids out shooting off firecrackers. They ease across the street trying not to let anyone see them. They stand by a dumpster and wait. Rick drives up exactly at 9:59.

When he got out he asked B-Money, "Where's your ride?" He walks over to shake their hands. Ice Man pulls out his .380 and stands behind him while B-Money steps back and pulls out his .357.

"Throw your money and gun on the ground," B-Money demanded.

"What is this all about?" Rick yells as he reaches in his pocket. He had about three g's on him. He tosses it along with his 9mm. B-Money tells him.

"After all we have been through how could you stab me in the back. Out of all people." Rick tries to play dumb like he didn't know what B-Money was talking about. But he knew that B-Money had found out about him and Strawberry.

"Strawberry!"

"You are gonna let a BITCH come between me and you?"

"It ain't about a bitch. It's about loyalty," B-Money said. Ice Man hits him hard in the back of the head with the pistol.

"This is for hitting me back in the day motherfucker." Then B-Money shot him in the head and threw some dope on the ground to make it look as if a drug deal had gone bad. The pair sneak back to the car. He pages Sheila and tells her to meet them at the club around 11:30. B-Money drops Ice Man back off at his apartment and he went home to freshen up. He chills with Strawberry for a minute and then let her know he had to take care of some business. Of course he left her some crack. When they arrive at the club they go in together. Back at the house Strawberry had the urge to page Rick but she was too scared. She wanted to tell him about B-Money finding out about him and her, but she gets high and forget about it. She feels it was her fault and knew there was nothing she could do about it.

Chapter 8

A few days later Rick's body was found. The investigators ruled it a homicide. When Strawberry saw it on the news, she knew B-Money had something to do with it. Now she was really scared of him. One night he came in so high he beat her because the house was not clean. He had been snorting and drinking a lot more than usual and his conscious was bothering him. He had shot someone before but he had never killed anyone. Every time he got high, he thought about putting a bullet in Strawberry. And she was thinking the same about him because she was tired of getting beat on. It was now 1994 and Ice Man had blown up big time. He had bought him a new jeep and B-Money had gotten him another house and a 92 Cadillac. Ice Man was also buying a house for him and Sheila and their three-year-old son. Tina was now working at a beauty salon and was living on her own. She would always check in on Grandma Mable and Strawberry was still getting high and being abused by B-Money. He had become very violent after murdering Rick. One night he was so drunk he beat her because she did not want to have sex with him. She was getting tired of his shit. She told him she was packing her belongings and leaving him. He puts the pistol to her head and tells her if she ever leaves him, he would kill her. She was so scared she didn't know what to do. B-Money went out of town one night, so Strawberry called an old friend of hers. He sold drugs, but he was not rolling like B-Money. She asked David if they could meet up somewhere. David was solo. He never ran with anyone and he sold his own dope. Nothing but quarters of crack. They meet up at McDonald's and she begins to tell David about all the money and dope B-Money has. She also let him know that B-Money beats on her and that she was tired of it and she was coming up with a plan to rob and kill him. On a cold winter night, Tina was coming in from seeing about Grandma Mable and a lady stops her.

"Excuse me. My name is Sara. I be seeing you with that guy in the Cadillac.

You know his name rings a bell. Do you know where I can get something?"

"Like what, Crack?" Tina said. "No, I don't have none but I will try and get

you some."

"Please," said the lady.

"We have to walk all the way across the tracks to get some and right now no one has any." She informs Tina that she lives in the complex and she would be there for a little while.

Tina calls B-Money on his cell, "Hey baby, I need a small bird."

He starts laughing, "You are crazy."

"No and I need it now." She hangs up. Thirty minutes later B-Money shows up. Tina tells him about the people in her apartment complex and that she needs to make her own money. He gives her an eight ball and shows her how to bag it up and gave her his old .38. When he left she went over to Sara's apartment. She lives with her sister Linda. Linda was also on crack. Linda was 31 with two kids, on welfare and she also receives child support. Sara was 28 with one child in Social Service's custody. He was 4 years of age. Sara left him home alone one night when he was 2-years old while she was out prostituting and someone called the police on her. She hasn't been right ever since. Tina's knock on the door brings Sara to open it. When she sees its Tina, she lets her in. Tina sold her two dimes for $15 and when they start smoking she left because they started looking funny to her. About two hours later, Sara came knocking on Tina's door. She had turned a trick and made $40 from sucking and fucking. This time she wanted four dimes. About two hours later she came back with her friend girl who was also a prostitute. This time they wanted five dimes. Finally, Tina got her some sleep. As she leaves out for work. she spots Sara hopping out of a car with a white man. So that's how she makes her money, Tina says to herself. Sara sees Tina and flags her down.

"Girl I need six dimes." Tina tells her to hop in and they hurry back to the house so that she could get to work. That Friday evening Sara had brought Tina so much business she was almost out of dope. Later that night, Tina meets B-Money at the club. She gives him a big kiss as he spots Sheila and Ice Man coming through the crowd. They had gotten her mother to babysit their son for them. As they walk out to the car to blaze a joint, Tina tells Sheila about all the money she has made. Tina kept her a big sack of weed. They went back in and had a few drinks and some hot wings and danced for a while. When the club closed, B-Money follows Tina to her place and Linda was waiting on her return. After Tina sells Linda the dope, she tells her she was done until the next day and she needed her to put the word out. Linda asked Tina to front her two bags and she would pay her later. Tina gives it to her. B-Money had been in the back snorting. Tina goes in the room and takes her clothes off and lays down beside B-Money. She kisses him on his neck and massages his penis. Then she slowly sucks his penis. She was trying to put it down her throat. Tina was a pro now when it came to sex and she was horny as hell. She laid on her back pulling him on top of her. She spreads her legs open and eases his penis inside of her. She enjoys him and not because she's been fucking him for years. It still hurt a bit when they fucked. Her vagina was so good and wet to him. He went deep as she moans and threw her ass back towards him like a boomerang. He hit it for a while until she gets on her knees wanting him to hit it from the back. She was crying but it felt so good to her. She bust a nut. As cum runs down the hairs of her vagina, Tina body shivers from the multiple orgasms. She could bust three before he gets his one. B-Money bust a nut in her and lays on his back. She cuddles up beside him and goes to sleep. The next morning when she wakes up, B-Money was gone. This made her mad because he didn't say a word. There was a knock at the door. It was Linda. She wanted to pay Tina for the two bags of dope she had gotten on credit. Plus, she wanted to buy three more, but Tina had only two left. So she sold them to her. She let Linda know it would be a few before she had some more. Tina had her some breakfast and calls B-Money.

"Hello. Why did you leave without saying goodbye?"

"I didn't want to wake you."

"Well I need a half egg."

"I have to go to Atlanta. I will drop it off about 2:00. Okay?" They hang up. B-Money moves Strawberry into his new house so he could have Tina over at his old one. Strawberry had found out about Tina years ago but she never pushed the issue with B-Money. After all these years Tina had no idea about Strawberry. It was 12:30 in the afternoon and B-Money tells Strawberry to get dressed and he would be back to pick her up. He wanted her to ride with him to Atlanta. He drops the dope off at Tina's and tells her he would probably see her later. Tina bags up the dope and goes over to Linda's afterwards to see what's up. There were people inside getting high and she was not afraid because she had her shirt pulled over her pistol. She sits in the living room while they smoked in the kitchen. Sara took a man in the bedroom for 30-minutes and came out with $25. She bought some dope from Tina and went in the room. Tina tells Linda to come outside and asked her if she would sell dope for her. Of course she said yes. Linda was not as bad off as Sara was. She knew when and when not to smoke. Tina took her over to her apartment and gave her $300 worth of dope.

"Bring me $230 and you keep $70." Tina was learning a lot about the dope game. Later Tina got dressed and went to the club. Sheila and Ice Man didn't show up. She had a few drinks and danced a little. Sunday morning, Linda had Tina's money. Later that evening, B-Money brought Tina a quarter. And then they got in an argument about her being in the club dancing with other guys. He snatches her by her collar and said, "You better not go no more without me." She agrees not to. The following week the police catches Ice Man with $5000 worth of dope on him. Sheila bails him out of jail and he chills for a few days. It was Christmas day and Tina spends the day with Grandma Mable. B-Money stops by for a while for them to exchange gifts. Then he returns home to spend the rest of the day with Strawberry. Tina went by to see her Aunt Alice and on the way home she goes by to see Sheila and Ice Man, who were spending Christmas with Sheila's mother.

Chapter 9

Another year had gone by and August 1, 1995 was a long boring day for Tina. Business was slow and B-Money had gone out of town. Tina was feeling like he had another woman on the side. She had felt this way for a while. However, she has never been able to catch him. She gets up to pour her a glass of gin and juice. She had seen people put crack in weed before. They call it, Judy Fly. She decides that she wanted to try it. It made her feel strong but it also made her feel good. Later that night, she puts it in a blunt. Then there was a knock at the door. It was Linda. She wanted a package. Tina gives her $300 worth and finishes her Judy Fly. B-Money came back early that morning and chills at Tina's place. He likes the way Tina handles things. Later, they went out for a bite to eat and rented some movies. A week later B-Money goes to the hole to drop a package off to one of his workers. It was dark and the streets were quiet. After he drops off the dope and heads back to his car two men behind a tree jumps him and shots him in the stomach. They take his money and jewelry. People rush outside to see what was going on but the two men had run off. B-Money was rushed to the hospital in stable condition. Someone reached out to Tina and told her what happened. She calls Sheila and Ice Man and they meet at the hospital. They were not able to go in his room just yet. So they chilled in the waiting room.

About two hours later, Strawberry shows up and goes into the room. A few minutes later the Dr. tells Tina, Ice Man and Sheila they could visit him now. When they get around the corner, Ice Man recognizes Strawberry. He tries to keep Tina from going into the room, but she felt something was wrong. When they walk in, Strawberry was kissing B-Money. Tina was so hurt she didn't know what to do. So she turns and walks out. Sheila went with her. Ice Man stays behind and talks to B-Money. Strawberry leaves the room. She wanted to find Tina and explain. And she did. She told Tina about everything. How they had been together for years and how he would beat her and threatened her if she ever tried to leave him. Tina could not believe what she was hearing, but on the other hand she felt Strawberry was telling the truth. She remembers how he choked her once. After they talked Tina went home and rolled up a Judy Fly. She smoked it and she rolls and smokes another one. Days had gone by and B-Money was home on bed rest. He calls Tina and gets no answer. This made him mad. Tina had started buying weight from Ice Man on the low. B-Money, was feeling a lot better and was ready to pay Tina a visit. He had been snorting and drinking again. Tina had not seen B-Money in three weeks. She even had changed the locks. This made him even madder that his key wouldn't fit.

So he knocks, "Who is it?"

"B-Money."

"What do you want?"

"We need to talk." So she let him in. They get into an argument about Strawberry and Tina told him it was over. He smacks her in the face twice and tells her she was his for life and she better not think about sleeping with anyone else, because he would kill her. B-Money walks out the door. Now she really believed Strawberry. When he left Tina's, he goes to the club and gets drunk. Afterwards, he drives home and jumps on Strawberry. He beats her so bad she had to go to the hospital for a broken rib. When they get there, they lied and said she fell down the stairs. The next day when he picks her up from the hospital he apologizes again for what he had done to her. He didn't know what had come over him. And she was tired of hearing the same old excuse. A few more months had come and gone and another Christmas was approaching and B-Money had taken Strawberry out of town with him and Tina was alone. She went over to Linda's house. Sara and Linda were home alone drinking a 40-ounce bottle of King Cobra Beer and a 5th of Night Train. Tina pulls out a few bags of crack and says,

"Well ladies, it's Christmas time and I'm sick and tired of that nigger." She was talking about B-Money. Then she asked, "Let me see that stem? How does this thing make you feel?"

"It will make you feel like you're on cloud nine." Linda said. That's where Tina wanted to go. The three ladies smoked and drank all night long. It was 7:00 AM the next morning when Tina finally went home. Feb. 1996, Tina found out she was two months pregnant. She had quit her job to sell dope fulltime. She and B-Money were still not getting along, but he was still hitting the vagina. One day she ran into Strawberry at the grocery store and they start talking about B-Money and how he treats them. They were tired of his bullshit. But they were both too scared of him and didn't know what else to do. Tina had gotten addicted to the stem and liked the way it made her feel. One night she was leaving Linda's apartment after getting high and found B-Money standing at her door, waiting on her to arrive.

"Where have you been?" She was so high she could hardly talk. When she got in the house he closes the door behind her.

He looks her in the eyes and said, "Bitch you been getting high!"

"No," she said with a twitching mouth. He smacks her so hard, she falls on the couch and said, "Bitch don't lie to me." He grabs her by her hair and slings her on the floor. Then he kicks her in her side and tells her, "You cannot have any more dope." She was in pain when he left. Tina he had Linda to drive her to the hospital. Once they got her settled in a room she shortly finds out she had a miscarriage. At first she was upset and then she felt it was for the best. She really didn't want B-Money's baby. Early the next morning, she was ready to leave the hospital and Linda was there for her. When she gets settled in at home she calls B-Money and lets him know what happened and if he ever came near her again she was going to call the police. She hangs up and packs a few clothes and stays at Grandma Mable's house for a few days. She didn't hear a peep out of B-Money. When she returns home she calls Ice Man for some dope. When he drops it off she bags it up and smokes some with Linda and Sara. The next day, things seemed to have gotten better for Tina. She chills and gets paid and wasn't worried about B-Money. She had made up her mind that if he came around she was going to shoot him. One night while B-Money was gone Strawberry started snooping around in the basement. That's where B-Money kept everything. She opens up the freezer and finds four-kilos of crack and six-ounces of powder. She goes upstairs to call David. She told him about the dope and how she was ready to set B-Money up. That Friday night, B-Money took Strawberry to the club. While at the club she sneaks out to give David a call. She asked him was he ready to take care of business. She gives him the address to B-Money's house and tells him that she had left the key under the trash can in the back. She went back in after hanging up with David and had a few drinks. While B-Money was getting his drink on and flirting with other women, back at the house David was hitting B-Money up for his stash. He was nervous, but he made it quick. Strawberry made it easy for him to get in and out. Everything was in place. He got the dope and left. When they got in from the club Strawberry started an argument. She did this on purpose. She had to hide his .357 under a pillow. When B-Money smacked her she fell on the bed and reaches under the pillow grabbing the gun.

"I'm tired of taking your shit B-Money!" When he reaches for the pistol, she shoots him in the chest. She cries while she calls the police. They took her down for questioning. She spills to the police that he was selling drugs. Which they already knew. Then she shows them the bruises on her body of how he had been beating on her. After a while they let her go. She took a cab to David's house. When she gets back in, she cries as she tells David why she had to kill him. They had a few drinks and ended the night with fucking. It has been some years since David had that vagina. The next morning, they split the dope. Strawberry felt like it was time for a change. So she left town and went home for a while. When Tina heard the news about B-Money's death she was hysterical. Sheila and Ice Man had to spend the day with her. Later that day, Sara and Linda filled in the gap. They shared a 5th of Gin and sipped and talked the night away. The day of the funeral Sheila, Ice Man and Tina went to view his body. B-Money was nicely dressed in a gray suit. When the family came in Tina sees her Aunt Alice near the front, being comforted by a man. Sheila looks at her as Tina thought to herself, B-Money couldn't be her son. She looks at the obituary and reads the names and sure as hell B-Money was her Aunt Alice's son. At that moment she wonders why she never mentioned him or had any pictures of him around in her house. Unless, he was the little boy in the picture with the afro. She never really gave it any attention. Then some girl starts singing Precious Lord. That's when Tina broke down crying. Sheila held her tight. Ice Man took it hard too but he tried his best to hold back the tears. But they ran down his face anyway. After the preacher eulogized the funeral the morticians rolled the casket out to the hearse. They drive to the gravesite but all Tina's thoughts were of disbelief, that Strawberry had killed B-Money. After the funeral Tina went home and calls her Aunt Alice and let her know she saw her at the funeral. Then she asked her why she didn't tell her that she had a son.

She told Tina, "Because you never asked. His father took B-Money from me when he was five years old. When he came back to me he was twelve. Then he started getting into all kinds of trouble. He quit school and started selling drugs at fifteen. He was rebellious. He hit me once and I put the police on him. Then I kicked him out the house. He hated me for that. But I hate that I never got the chance to tell him that I love him." In Tina's mind, she was thinking the same thing.

Then she asked Tina, "How did you know my son?"

Tina replied, "I used to see him around." When Tina gets off the phone she thought, Damn I slept with my first cousin for all these years and didn't even know it. And then she breaks down crying again. Tina smokes Judy Flies, indulge in cups of Gin and cries until she falls asleep.

Chapter 10

Months had gone by and Tina was not doing too well in the dope business. She was smoking more than she was selling. One night she went to the club and met a drug dealer name Jeff. They start off having a good conversation over drinks. Then Jeff follows her home. When they get in they smoke a joint. Tina allows him to kiss her and then she asked if he knew where she could get a half of an ounce. He gave her his cell number to give him a call. Tina and Sheila were not talking as much because Tina was too busy getting high. She didn't even go see Grandma Mable that much. Later that evening, she gives Jeff a call and he brought her over the half-ounce. Then he asked her if he could take her out later. But she claims she would be busy.

"So what about tomorrow?" He asked.

"Call me." So he left. Tina bags up her dope and heads over to Linda's house. There were a few people already getting high. She decides to go see Grandma Mable. When Grandma lays eyes on Tina she was very happy.

She told her, "Come in and have a seat." After they finish talking, Grandma Mable asked Tina, "Why are you losing weight?"

"I don't know." Tina replied.

"You need to start eating more." Later she goes home and smokes her a Judy Fly. Since Linda had company, she didn't feel comfortable with smoking around anyone else. Unless it was Sara. She lays on the couch and starts thinking about B-Money while listening to the radio. She thought about how sweet he was when she first met him. Then she drifts off to sleep. The next day Jeff calls and asked her out again and she finally said yes. Jeff seemed like a nice guy and he was very handsome. When they get back to her place, he kisses her and drives off because it was getting late. She stops by Linda's and she had sold all of Tina's dope. Tina goes home to get some more and returns back to Linda's apartment. They sit at the kitchen table and smoke a piece. Later, Sara comes in with Paul. He was surprised to see Tina sitting there. As he spoke, Tina could not believe her eyes. She had not seen Paul in a couple of years. He had on some dingy pants and a pair of worn out shoes that looked as if it had come out of Family Dollars. Paul had lost everything. His wife, kids, car and his job. He had nothing but a bad habit. Then Sara wanted to know if Tina had four dimes. Tina sold her the dope and Sara and Paul went into another room. Tina gave Linda a bag to smoke for herself because she did not want Paul to catch her smoking. Sara kept coming out for more dope. Tina moved to the living room. After a while, Paul and Sara had moved to the table. They were still smoking and buying. Before she knew it Paul had spent $250 with her and now he was out of money. So Tina fronts him two dimes and she leaves. Tina had been seeing Jeff for three weeks now. She was kind of falling for him. He took her out to dinner and then they went to the club for a couple of drinks. They ended up leaving early so they came back to her place. She told him to have a seat and that she would be right back. She took Linda a package so she wouldn't be disturbed. When she gets back, in she pulls Jeff off the couch and took him to her bedroom. She takes her clothes off and crawls on top of him. As she takes off his clothes, she starts kissing him. She clutches his penis and sticks it in her mouth. She lays on her back and grabs her ankles. Jeff couldn't believe it. However, he rests between her thighs and put his penis inside of her. They were rolling in rhythm with one another. Her vagina was wet and Jeff was enjoying every minute of it. He flips over and lets her ride him. She was moaning while she bounces up and down on his penis. He puts her on all fours and she nuts all on his penis. She was good, Jeff thought to himself. She lays on her back and wraps her legs around his waist and they begin to slow grind and the sensation was feeling so good to Jeff. They both bust a nut at the same time. They wipe off and then Jeff tells Tina that he had to go. Tina didn't like that Jeff could not spend the night. The next day Tina calls Jeff but she didn't get an answer. She calls him again later that night, still no answer. Tina began to feel like she had been played. Then she remembers how it was when she was with B-Money. So she hits up Sheila and asked her if she wanted to go to the mall. Tina picks her up around 4:00 that evening and they head to the mall. After shopping they grab a bite to eat. A few days later, Tina meets Ice Man to pick up some dope. After leaving, just a block away from home, she is pulled over by an officer. She spots a half of a joint in the ashtray. The officer calls for a female cop to come out. They search Tina and her car and find dope. She was taken to jail and Sheila was called and she bails Tina out. Two days later she goes to court and was placed on three-years' probation because she did not have a prior arrest record. A month had passed and Tina was out of pocket. She had been hitting Grandma Mable up for gram money to stay on. But she was smoking too heavy to get all the way up. One night she called Ice Man and told him she needed to see him but don't tell Sheila. Later on, Ice-Man stops by. When he arrives, Tina was sitting on the couch wearing a short nightgown. She tells him she was out of pocket and she needs some dope to pay her bills.

"How much do you need?"

"About a half of ounce."

"That's a lot of dope for you not to have any money. I know we are friends and all but damn Tina." Tina lay back on the couch and spreads her legs with no panties in sight. She extends her legs even more as she motions for him to come closer. He takes off his clothes and inserts his penis inside of her. She was tight. She hadn't had sex in a while. Then she asked him to get up and go in the room. She edges up on the bed with her ass tooted in the air and he sticks it in from the back. Tina starts crying but she rolls that ass all on Ice Man's penis. She was telling him how good it feels. She lays on her back and places her legs on his shoulders, as he positions his penis back inside of her tight vagina. She was rolling and screaming telling him to beat it. Tina was real wet and horny. She had bust two nuts. They had been going at it for an hour and a half. Then he came inside of her. She didn't want to let him up.

He kisses her and tells her he had to get back home. He cleans up and on his way to the door he feels her vagina and said, "Damn girl its good. I will drop that off in the morning." When he left Tina was still horny. She could not believe how good Ice Man penis was and he knew how to use it and she knew she had to have it again. The next morning, Sheila went out looking for another house. They felt like their spot was getting a little too hot. So Ice Man calls Tina and tells her he's on his way. As he drives towards Tina's house he thinks about last night and how good it was and at the same time she was thinking the same thing. She had showered and put on her see through lingerie. When he came to the door he gave Tina the dope and she hid it. Then she yanks him to the room and pushes him down on the bed and kisses him. He removes her panties to the side and rubs the hairs on her vagina. When she was good and wet they take their clothes off. He fucked Tina all kinds of ways and she allowed him to.

After he came in he tells her, "This cannot happen again."

"I know." Tina said. So they agreed that this was the last time and they fuck again. When they finished he washes up and leaves. Tina gets up and showers again. She knew in her mind, that what she was doing was wrong. But she was too far caught up in the game. This day and age she was willing to do anything to stay on. Even if it meant to keep fucking Ice Man. She got dressed and went over to Linda's place, smokes a joint and bags up her dope. She sits around all day and made $120. It was a slow day. Then she leaves Linda with a package and goes over to see her Grandma. She sat and talked a while and fixed herself a plate. Tina left Grandma's and chilled for the rest of the night. She didn't even want to smoke any dope.

CHAPTER 11

It was a Saturday night, Tina gets dressed and goes to the club. Sheila and Ice Man were already there when she arrives. They kick it like nothing had happened between them. He bought the ladies drinks and even winks at Tina when Sheila wasn't looking. And she graciously smiles back at him. Tina spots Jeff from across the room looking at her. He turns away like he did not see her and continues talking to a woman near the bar. Feeling good from all the Hennessey she had consumed, Tina walks over to Jeff.

"I know you saw me sitting over there."

"What's up?" Jeff said.

"Why you don't return my calls."

"I don't know what you're talking about." The woman that Jeff was having a conversation with was his wife. So she chimes in. "Jeff who is this bitch? And what the fuck is she talking about?" She smacks Tina and a fight breaks out in the club. After the fight Tina went home and got high.

The next morning, Linda was out of dope. Tina gave her some more. She took the money and purchased money orders for all her bills. Then she calls Ice Man.

"Can you front me a half," She asked. The next morning, he took her what she asked for. They made love this time because the both of them now had grown up feelings for each other. The year 1998 had come in and Tina was at it again. She took Linda, Sheila and Sara out to a bar one night for drinks. It wasn't a classy bar, just somewhere to hang out for a drink. It was a Thursday night and a few guys were flirting with the ladies. One guy asked Sara if she wanted to dance. So she did. He looked as if he had some money. After the dance they all had a few more drinks until Tina was ready to go. Linda and Sheila left with Tina but Sara stayed with the guy she danced with. The man bought Sara more drinks and asked her what she was doing for the rest of the night.

"Going home with you if you got some money." Sara was so drunk she didn't know if she was in a blue or a black Cadillac. He rides down a dark road, parks, gets out and goes over to the passenger side.

"Get out and get in the back seat." She did what he said.

"Take you clothes off."

"I have to have the money first!" She demanded.

"I have it," He replied, as he feels her vagina.

"Stop and give me the money!"

He pulls out his pistol, "I said get naked." She was so scared she asked no more questions. He takes his pants down and grabs her by her head. He made her suck his penis for about ten minutes.

"Lay back in the seat." She cries as she begs the man not to kill her.

"Cooperate and I won't." Sara lays back and spreads her legs as he sticks his fingers in her to test the wetness. As she lays back with tears in her eyes, he slides his penis inside of her. He fucks her for 30 minutes and made her suck his penis again. He was getting ready to cum. She could feel it. But she kept sucking. He nuts in her mouth and puts her out the car on the dark road. She begs him to take her back to the bar. He drops her off close by and gives her $5. She walks the rest of the way home. It wasn't her first time being raped and she knew it was a price to pay when she prostituted. When she gets home she tells Linda what happened. She was mad. Mostly for Sara, because she hated what her sister was doing. She expressed to her time and time again about prostituting. Linda was afraid Sara was going to get killed in the streets. Then she gives her some crack. Tina was still getting high but she was keeping herself up. With the exception of her losing weight. She didn't have time for a real relationship because she spent all her free time getting high. She would go weeks without sex unless Ice Man was fucking her. One cold night, Sara came knocking on Tina's door cold and shivering.

"Come in girl. What the hell you doing out there like that with that little ass jacket on?"

"Trying to get high," Sara said as she pulls out a 5th of Gin. "Damn! Tina said. Just what I need." She goes to the kitchen and grabs two glasses and a can of Sprite out of the refrigerator. Sara pulls out $25 and tells Tina to give her three. Tina had on her short gown. Sara told her how much she liked it. They sit on the couch and get high. Over half of the Gin was gone, Tina took a shell hit and lays back. Sara rubs on Tina. She pulls her panties to the side and licks her. Tina was shell, she did not know what to think. But it felt good. Sara took her tongue and licks her clit as she inserts her fingers inside of Tina. Tina closes her eyes and holds Sara by her ears, spreading her legs wider as she slowly rolls her butt. Nobody ever ate Tina vagina the way Sara was eating it. About 20 minutes later Tina was about to cum. She pushes Sara's hands back but Sara moves her hands and keeps licking. After Tina bust her nut she articulates to Sara she better not tells no one about what happened.

"Have you ever been with a woman before?"

"No." Sara replied.

"Why me?"

"Because you are beautiful and I like your personality."

"Thank you." Tina said.

"But you are a pretty girl too Sara." Tina twist up a blunt and they finish off the Gin. They were both drunk, doing a lot of talking. Then Sara kisses Tina and takes her clothes off. Tina looks at Sara's body and sees it was nicer than hers. Sara was short and thick with a firm round ass. They go into Tina's bedroom, kissing and fondling each other's vagina. Afterwards, they went to sleep. The next morning, they take a shower and get dressed and Sara goes home to put on clean clothes. While cooking breakfast, Tina calls Ice Man. He came over to drop her some dope off and left. He had people helping him and Sheila move into their new place. After bagging up her dope, Tina went over to Linda's house. She gave Linda a package and went back home. She was tired and needed to take a nap. Thursday morning Sheila asked Tina if she wanted to go to the mall. Tina agrees. When Sheila picks up Tina, she pays attention to the funny color lipstick she has on. She remembers Ice Man had that same color on his collar. When he asked him where it came from, he said he bumped into a waitress at a restaurant. She didn't want to jump to conclusions, so she said nothing. At the mall Sheila was talking to Tina about things between her and Ice Man but Tina kept jumping off the subject. In Sheila's mind she knew that Ice Man and Tina would not stoop that low. After shopping and eating Sheila drops Tina back off at her place. Tina did not spend much money at the mall this time. Later that day, she collects some money from Linda. She made $150.

"Where is Sara?" Tina asked.

"She went to the store." Tina went back home and gave Grandma Mable a call. Friday night Ice Man hooks up with a guy name Fast Freddy who wants to sell dope for him. He gave Fast Freddy a package and then went home to spend a quiet Friday night with Sheila. After he relaxes, he fires up a blunt. He starts rubbing on her vagina. Sheila asked him to stop because she was not in the mood. She could not stop thinking about the lipstick on his collar.

"What is wrong?" Iceman asked.

But she said, "Nothing."

He cuddles up with her and they watch the movie. The next morning Ice Man calls Tina to see if she was out of dope. He really wanted some vagina. She told him not yet and that she would call him later. When she got off the phone she went over to Linda's. Linda had company. There were two guys and a lady that looked as if they had been up all night.

"Linda are you out of dope?" Tina asked.

"Yes, but I am $15 short." Tina didn't get mad. She knew the first of the month was around the corner and Linda always paid her debts. Tina told them she had a few bags on her if they needed more. But they were out of money. One of the guys had a gold ladies ring he was trying to sell. Tina had no interest in it. She had enough of jewelry. Plus, she needed the money. The man went to the pawn shop while Tina waited. He came back in twenty-five minutes and he was back with $35. She gave him five dimes and left. Now, she was ready to call Ice Man. About an hour later, Sara shows up with a guy. She bought two dimes and takes him in the room. About 30 minutes later she came out and wanted four more. Tina only had three. Tina calls Ice Man for a re-up. When he gets there with the package, she was short as usual with her part. But he didn't care. He kisses her and plays in her vagina.

"Can I stop by later?" Ice Man asked.

"No. I want to be alone." He left a little upset, but he had to go check on Fast Freddy. Tina didn't want him to stop by later because she had her fresh package and she wanted to get high. Tina bags up the dope and takes Linda a three pack. She sits around for a couple of hours and then she goes back home. She pours a shot of Gin and rolls up a Judy Fly. When she was high and alone, she found herself in thought about B-Money. She turns on the radio to block the distraction. Then there was a knock at the door. It was Sara. She tells Tina she needs someone to talk too. She didn't even want to get high. They sit down and talk. Sara was tired. She had been running the streets for two days, sucking and fucking to get high. She confessed to Tina the tricks she had turned for twelve years. She told her about how she had been beat and raped. Sara was in tears. Tina hugs her and gives her a kiss on the cheek.

"Go take a shower and go get in my bed." Tina said to Sara. When Sara gets out of the shower she joins Tina in the bed. She calls for her to come and hold her. Tina agrees and Sara was asleep in five minutes. Tina kisses her on the forehead and covers her up. She went to smoke her a Judy Fly and listens to the Quiet Storm, until she falls asleep. Tina prepares her and Sara some late morning brunch. They had bacon, eggs and French toast. Tina showers and lays in the bed.

She tells Sara, "I am not getting high today. All I want to do is chill with you." It was Sunday and it had been a long time since the ladies had relaxed and not got high.

Chapter 12

Tina and Sara had become very close. Sara didn't turn as many tricks as she used to because Tina would look out for her when she could. She tried to keep Sara around as much as she could. Tina was out riding around one day and she saw a girl she knew that smokes dope.

"Hey Tonya."

"Hey Tina. What's up?"

"I need you to do me a favor if you don't mind."

"No, what is it?"

"I need you to go in the Video News Store and buy me a nice size dildo."

Tonya agrees. When they pull up Tina gives her a $50 bill. Tonya goes in and out within minutes.

"Here is your change." Tonya said.

"That didn't take long." Tina said.

Tina drives in Tonya's parking lot and gives her a dime and points to Linda's apartment.

"If you need something that's where to go." They get out of the car and go their separate ways. As she opens the box she laughs. She was thinking how funny it was. She takes her pants off and lay in the bed and spread her vagina lips with her fingers and rubs her clit with the dildo. She eases the dildo in a little at a time, going in and out. Then she starts to roll her ass around while she pushes and pulls the dildo in and out. It didn't feel as good as a real man being on top of her, but it was doing the trick. She puts her legs in the air and plunges the dildo up and down in her vagina as hard as she could. She went deep and starts to moan. It felt so good, she did it for a while. She even imagined B-Money fucking her for the first time. After she got a nut she said to herself, I hope my baby enjoys this. She was talking about Sara, but Sara was nowhere to be found that day or night. So the next night, she goes to Linda's to see how much money she had made. It wasn't much but she got what she had.

"Is Sara home?"

"No." Linda said. Tina went back home. Later, Sara arrives at Tina's door. She was tired. So she showers and lays down with Tina. Tina did not say a word. The summer had rolled around and Tina was watching the 5:00 news. They were talking about a guy that was killed at a convenient store. His name was not released. About 20 minutes later, Sheila calls to let her know that Paul had been killed trying to rob a store. Some of the customers said he was drunk and pointing a gun at the people inside the store. The owner came from the back of the store with a gun and shot Paul in the head. He died on the scene. It was the weekend and business was booming at Linda's. Tina and Sara were upstairs at Tina's getting high. After they got to their levels, Tina wanted Sara to have sex with her. Sara wanted more dope. Tina would not give it to her. Sara got mad and curses Tina out. Tina begins to cry. Her sensitivity revealed that she had fallen in love with Sara. All Sara knew was the streets. She didn't know anything about love or loving anyone else. Sara left out the door mad as hell. Tina calls Ice Man but he was busy and could not stop by. Tina was mad. She was high and she wanted to be fucked. She lays on the bed with the music down low. She takes out her dildo and plunges it in and out of her vagina. Hell, it wasn't even pleasing her. She wanted to be comforted and held by someone. She got up and went back over to Linda's to see what was going on. There were a few people spending money. Tina took the money that Linda had made and gave her the dope she had on her. Tina sat in the living room. It had gotten late and then Sara came through the door with $60 that she had made. Before she had a chance to spend it, Tina grabs her by the hand and takes Sara to her apartment. They got into a big argument. Sara tried to go out the door but Tina grabs her. Sara snatches away and Tina smacks her. She smacks Tina back. Tina sits on the couch and cries as Sara goes back out the door. Sara goes back to her sister's house and buys some dope. She was looking upset when Linda saw her.

"What was that all about?" Linda asked.

"Nothing," Sara said, as she sits down at the table and gets high.

The next evening, Tina goes over to collect from Linda. When she gets in, she observed that Linda had a new TV and VCR that some guy had sold her. Linda was not trying to smoke up all of her profits. She even bought her kids some new clothes.

"Where is Sara?" Tina asked.

"Asleep. What was up with you and my sister last night?"

"Nothing. We are just friends." Tina walks out leaving Linda thinking it was more to it than they were willing to tell. Tina calls Ice Man for a half a bird. He tells her he would be there shortly. When he arrives he wanted to kiss Tina. But she was still mad. Ice Man grabs her by the ass and asked her if he could see her later. She said maybe and then he left. Tina bagged up her dope and took Linda a package. When Tina arrives, Sara was sitting at the table. They made eye contact and smile after greeting one another.

"Girl do you want to go and get something to eat?"

"Yes. Let me shower and put on some clothes." Sara said. Tina went upstairs to her apartment to wait on Sara. When Sara got out the shower she put on a new outfit she had bought from a man on the street. It was hugging all of her curves. Then here comes Linda with the questions.

"What is up between you and Tina?"

"None of your business." Sara left out to go up to Tina's place. Once inside, they hug and swap apologies.

"I'm tired of you running the streets," Tina said to Sara as they sit down on the couch.

"I am tired of running in the streets. I really care about you. I love you and I will stop tricking." They went to dinner. Sara even paid for the meal. She didn't spend all of her money last night because she was too upset to get high. Tina and Sara arrive back around 9:00 PM. They stop by the ABC Store on the way home for a 5th of

Hennessey. They wanted to chill together for the rest of the night. They fixed a drink and went in the bedroom. Tina rolls up a blunt and Sara gets naked and lay across the bed. She wanted to catch the 9:00 movie, Sugar Hill. It was one of her favorites. In the middle of the movie, Tina gets up to fix them another drink. At the end of the movie Tina pulls out the dildo.

"What the hell is that?" Sara hollered.

"What do it look like?" Tina smiles, as she throws the in motion vibrator on Sara. Tina takes her clothes off and the pair made love for hours. Afterwards, they cuddle and watched The Late Show. Two months had gone by and Tina and Sara were in love. Linda knew what was going on between the two, but she didn't care. Sara stayed at Tina's house more often and Tina had stopped sleeping with Ice Man. They only did business together and that was it. But she would allow him to kiss her every now and then. Her heart belonged to Sara now. Plus, Sheila had questioned her about Ice Man. One-night Ice Man got drunk and wanted to fuck Sheila but she wouldn't give him any. He storms out the house mad at 1:15 in the morning. He goes over to Tina's house, beating on her door until she opens it.

"Who is it?"

"Ice-Man."

"I'm sleep." Tina said.

"It's an emergency." Ice Man replied. When she opens the door he tries to kiss her. She knew he was drunk. He tells her how much he needs her. Sara came out the bedroom and said, "Who is he and what the hell going on?"

"Nothing. He was leaving." Tina said.

"Ice-Man shouted, "Who the fuck is you?"

"I am Tina's girlfriend." Then there was a knock at the door.

"Who is it?" Tina yelled.

"Sheila, BITCH! Open the door!" When Tina opens the door Sheila curses them out some more. At the same time Sara was putting on her clothes. Sheila swings on Tina but Ice Man jumps in between them.

"Bitch I knew you were fucking my man." That's all Sara needed to hear. Sara went out the door, Sheila follows and Ice Man did the same. All Tina could do was sit on the couch and cry. She knew she had to get dressed and find Sara. She did not want her to go out and get high. She knocks on Linda's door.

"Is Sara here?"

"I thought she was with you?" Linda replied. Tina left and got in her car. She drove around looking for Sara, but Sara was nowhere to be found. When Sara left the apartment there were two guys in the parking lot getting high. They asked her if she wanted to get high. She accepted their invitation and got in the car. They rode around to the back of the building. They let her hit the dope and asked her what she would do for a twenty. She told them she would suck their penis. One of the guys wanted her vagina instead. When they gave her the dope she got naked. She put one of the guy's penis in her mouth while the other one hit her from behind. When they were done they let her out and she walks around to the front of the complex. She went back to Tina's house. Tina let her in and Sara asked her if she wanted to hit it. Tina declined and went in her bedroom. When Sara finished getting high she got in the shower. Tina could not sleep so she lounges and listens to music. When Sara returned from her shower, she came and got in the bed with Tina. She didn't know what to say. She felt embarrassed and ashamed. Tina was mad but she was glad that Sara was back. Tina had her back turned to Sara. She could not look at her because of what she had done.

Sara hugs Tina and said, "I'm sorry."

"Don't pull that shit again," Tina said.

Then she explains to Sara why she had slept with Ice Man. She let her know when things started to get serious she backed up off of him. Now that Sara knew the truth, she felt a lot better. They agreed that they would not cheat on one another and went off to sleep. Sara had practically moved in with Tina. The only time she stayed out is when she went downstairs to get high with her sister. At this point they had built up trust.

CHAPTER 13

It was Sunday morning and after breakfast Tina and Sara lounge around the house. It was 2:00 and Grandma Mable was home from church. So Tina gives her a call.

"Hey Grandma."

"Hey sweetie."

"Whatcha doing?" Tina asked.

"Nothing. Getting ready to cook."

"Good. I want you to cook enough for me and my friend."

"Ok." Grandma said.

"I will see you in a little while," Tina said and then they ended their call. Tina told Sara she wants her to meet her grandma. However, she needs her to act like they were just friends. Sara did not like that.

"So behind closed doors I'm your lover, but in public I'm just your friend?"

"No. It's not like that. I need some time to spring something like this on my Grandma."

"It's not only your Grandma I'm talking about Tina. Last week when we were at the restaurant I wanted to hold your hand. But you played it off by pointing at that damn picture. Then I wanted to kiss you and you said not right now."

"Like I said Sara, I need time." Sara got up and put on her clothes and tramps out the room. Tina jumps up and run behind her. She grabs Sara and threw her on the couch.

"Don't you do this to me, I love you." Tina said.

Sara pushes Tina off of her and said, "If you love me then work on changing then." Tina takes Sara by the hand and leads her back to the bedroom. She takes off Sara's clothes and lays her back on the bed. They kiss and play with each other's vaginas. Tina gently licks Sara from her neck to her nipples. She kisses her way down to her stomach until she gets to her vagina. Sara spreads her legs wide. Tina licks around her spare tongue while her two fingers are inside of her. It felt so good to Sara. She rolls her pretty ass in slow motion.

"Take your fingers out and just eat it." Tina did what was asked of her. When Sara reaches her climax she pulls Tina back on top of her and they start kissing some more. Sara flips Tina on the bottom. It was her opportunity to return the favor. She sucks on Tina as she digs in her vagina. Nobody ate Tina's vagina like Sara did. When Sara starts sucking on Tina's vagina she closes her eyes. Sara always made Tina moan. That's how good she was. When it was time for her to bust she pulls Sara up and gives her a hug.

"Baby don't leave me. You know I need you in my life." Tina whispers.

"I need you too Tina. More than you will ever know." About an hour later they take a shower together and got dressed. They stop by Linda's to see what she was doing. Linda and the kids were watching TV. They let Linda know they were going over to Grandma's house. Linda was almost out of dope. She gave Tina what she had made off the dope and asked her if she could take her to the grocery store. On the way to the grocery store Tina asks Linda, "Why you don't have a man?"

"Every man that I've dated did drugs or was abusive. I figured I would wait on Mr. Right." Linda replied.

"That could take forever." Tina laughed.

Then Linda asked, "What is it like being a lesbian?"

"You say it like it's a bad thing." Tina said.

"No, I just don't see you being with my sister."

"Well your sister is a sweet person. As long as she is not running the streets."

"I know that." Linda said. When they arrive at the grocery store Tina stays in the car while Linda goes inside. A guy approaches Tina while she's sitting in the car waiting on her to come out the store.

"Hey, how are you doing?"

"Fine," she said looking at him up and down. He was fine, tall and built. He had waves swimming in his freshly cut hair and a gold tooth his mouth.

"So who are you waiting on?" He asked.

"My friend."

"So are you married?" He probed.

"No." She answered.

"You have a boyfriend?"

"No." He hands Tina his business card and tells her to call him sometime.

By this time Linda was coming back, so she hurries and puts the card in her pocket. Linda gets in the car and asked Tina, "Who was that good looking guy you were talking too? Yeah, be honest." Linda said.

"To be honest I don't know. I did not get his name." They go back to the house to drop Linda off. After Linda makes her last trip from the car, Tina tells Linda to tell Sara to come on. On the ride to Grandma Mable's house they got in deep conversation about love. Sara asked Tina if she loved her enough to marry her.

Tina laughed it off adding, "Are you serious?"

"I'm not joking." Sara said.

Then Tina got serious. "You are for real?"

"Yeah." Sara responded.

"You know people of the same sex cannot get married here in North Carolina."

"But what if we could? Would you marry me?" Tina pulls into Grandma's driveway, parks and looks at Sara.

"Yes, I love you enough to marry you." Then she sneaks her a kiss. They get to the door and Grandma Mable opens it after the first knock and gives Tina a hug.

"Come in." Grandma said. "Have a seat." They sit and talk for a while. Sara asked Grandma Mable if she had a scrapbook with pictures of Tina when she was a baby. And she did. She showed Sara a lot of Tina's pictures. Sara was telling Tina how pretty she was. They wash up for dinner around 5:00 PM. Grandma Mable cooked meatloaf, black-eyed peas, collard greens, rice and cornbread and sweet tea to wash it down. After they ate they sit in front of the TV to watch the 6:00 evening news. When the news went off Grandma Mable excused herself to the bathroom. Tina feels Sara's titties and they both laugh. It was getting late in the evening and Tina was ready to go. On her way out Grandma Mable kisses her and tells her to come back to see her. When they pull up to their apartment complex they spot an unmarked car. It was the Vice Squad. They pull off. Tina goes in and she tells Sara to go get the dope from Linda. Sara tells Linda about the vice outside lurking. For the rest of the day everyone chilled. Tina had a half of Gin and her and Sara drank and smoked blunts. She hid the rest of the dope just in case. They chilled on the couch and listened to music and smoked until they were ready for bed. When Tina took her pants off, the card she had in her pocket fell out. She had forgotten all about it. When Sara came out the bathroom Tina was laying down. Sara picks up the card and goes into the living room and calls the number on the card. His name was Mike.

When he answers, Sara asked, "Do you know a girl name Tina?"

"I met her today at the store."

"Did she tell you that she had a girlfriend?"

"No. What do you mean by that?"

"I'm fucking the bitch." And she hangs up.

The whole time Tina is sitting at the edge of the bed. Sara storms in the room.

"Let me explain." Tina said. He just handed me his number and I forgot to throw it away."

"So why didn't you tell him you had a girlfriend?"

"It's not that easy to let the whole world know that I'm gay Sara. I keep telling you it's going to take me some time."

"Well I'm going to give you some time." Sara went for the door and Tina just let her leave. Sara went to Linda's. She could talk to her sister about anything. She empties all of her feelings out to Linda. Linda could not believe what she was hearing. She knew they were fucking around but she had no idea all of what she was hearing was going on. She had no clue that they were in love. Linda told her to go lay down and go back to Tina's in the morning. Sara lays on the couch thinking about Tina. Meanwhile, Tina was upstairs about to go crazy worrying about Sara. In her mind, she knew Sara was going to go out and fuck for some dope. She was hurt. She was tired of running behind Sara but she finally dozes off to sleep. The next morning, Tina goes to Linda's house. Sara opens the door. Linda was still asleep.

"I can't believe that you are here." Tina said.

"And why not?" Sara sarcastically replied.

"I figured you would still be out on the whore stroll."

"Girl please." Sara laughed.

"Get up and come home and eat breakfast with me."

Tina went into Linda's room and gave her a package and then Tina and Sara left to go back to her place. Linda had sold all of the dope she had. Tina calls Ice Man to re-up.

"Where is your girl?" Ice Man asked.

"She's in the room."

"What happened Tina?"

"Well we started out as friends and then we became close. She was here for me. Now are you going to bring the half?"

"Yeah, I will do that for you. Look here lil mama. You know you are going to have to let me have that ass one last time."

"Whatever," she said smiling. Sara just laughs and shakes her head.

"It's only business baby." Tina said. Soon Ice Man was there. Sara was sitting on the couch as Tina went to the back to get the money.

"I need it all today." Ice Man said.

"I will have it in a little while." Tina replied.

"Well I can't do it." And he left. About an hour later Ice Man calls Tina. "Hey you still need that?"

"Yes."

"Meet me at Corey's house. You know where he stays don't you?"

"Yeah. You talking about Corey that used to sell for B-Money right?"

"Yeah," he said and hung up. Tina went to see if she could get a hundred dollars from Grandma Mable. When she arrives at Corey's house Ice Man was there waiting. Corey was gone and Tina already knew what was up. He had the half-ounce in his hand.

"Come on in nigga and make it quick." She plops on the couch and took Ice Man's penis out. Then she sucks it. About five minutes later he says stop. He gives her the dope and she hands him money.

"You are a good girl Tina. Plus, you are my friend. I am not going to play you for no dope."

"Thank you," she said.

"But if you and that sexy ass girlfriend of yours decide to have a threesome. Let me know." Tina left without saying a word. When she got home she sat at the table to cut up the dope.

"Did you get the money from your Grandma?" Sara asked.

"No. I just had to meet Ice-Man."

"I know you didn't fuck him for it?"

"No sweetie. He tried me. But he ended up giving it to me. Then he said if we ever wanted to have a threesome let him know."

"Shit!" Sara said. "You should have told him to bring it on." Tina looked at her with a crazy frown on her face.

"Just kidding baby." Sara said as she kisses her. Sara went into the room and Tina finished bagging up the dope and took Linda a package.

Chapter 14

Weeks went by since the blow up between Sheila and Tina. Tina settles to give Sheila a call but she didn't answer. She left two voicemail messages but Sheila didn't respond. She regrets what she had done and was feeling guilty about it. Sheila was her best friend. They were like sisters and she allowed the dope to take that away. Sheila moved back home with her mother and had started back working. Her mother helped her get on at Lance Snacks. She didn't want anything to do with Ice Man nor Tina. She could not believe they had done her like this. When Ice Man came to see his son. Sheila would send him out the door. She didn't even speak. After a month working at Lance, Sheila bought her a car. She was doing well for herself. She no longer smoked pot. Sheila pulls up to the BP to get some gas. Ice Man pulls up behind her. He wanted a hug and a kiss. She wouldn't give it to him. So he punches her in the eye. The store manager calls the police. But he had already gone before they arrived. The cops asked her to go downtown to file a warrant against Ice Man. The two cops knew Ice Man by heart. They had busted him one time before.

"Do he sell dope?" One officer asked.

"I don't know. I separated from him and that is why he hit me." Three weeks later Ice Man was on his way to deliver some dope to Fast Freddy and Corey. The same two cops spot his car. They put the blue light on him but he smashes the gas. They stay behind him as he speeds up. There were more police cars in on the chase. Ice-Man was doing 70 mph. As he makes a sharp turn, he hits a little boy that is outside playing. Ice Man is in shock in. He didn't know what to do. He wanted to move but his feet wouldn't. And he was surrounded by cops.

"Get out the car with your hands on your head!" The cop hollers. When he gets out the car they rush him to the ground. Minutes later Channel 9 News and Channel 3 News were on the scene. Ice Man was taken to jail. He was charged with reckless driving, failure to stop, possession of a firearm and two ounces of crack and hitting a pedestrian. He was placed under a $500,000 bond. The little boy was rushed to the hospital where he later died. The next day his bond was revoked. His charges were elevated to manslaughter and his case was indicted by the grand jury. He calls Sheila later that day to let her know what had happened. She expected his call.

"I need you to do me a favor. Collect my money from Fast Freddy and Corey and go to my house and go to my stash and get the rest of my money and find me a lawyer." She did it for him. She found Ice Man a lawyer and a few days later he went to see him and got him in court. The lawyer asked for him a bond and the judge gave him the $500,000 bond back. Sheila was in court for support. That evening Sheila receives another call from Ice-Man.

"Look here Sheila I need you to sell everything I own." He knew money was not going to buy him freedom but he wanted a lesser plea than what they were offering him. In a week Sheila had sold everything Ice Man owned and paid the lawyer with every dime. Ice Man was looking at 35 years to life. Meanwhile, Tina did not have any connections. So she talked to a guy who bought dope from Linda because he knew a man that sold weight. He hooked Tina up with the guy Rusty, also known as Big Daddy. When he stops by Tina's apartment he likes what he sees. He even made a pass at her but she was not interested in him. He was real dark and weighed about 300 pounds. She bought the dope and asked him to leave. After she bags it up, she notices that she didn't get as many dimes as she used to get from Ice Man. But she still gave Linda her $300 package. When she got to Linda's, Sara was sitting at the table with two guys smoking. Tina did not like it one bit. She looks at her with the evil eye and gives Linda the dope and leave. About five minutes later Sara was behind her. She was shell and sits on the couch. Tina pours herself a drink and smokes a blunt. Sara asked Tina for some dope but she said no and for her to watch TV and chill. Sara was not trying to hear that. She tries to leave but Tina stands in front of the door. Sara pushes Tina out of the way and opens the door.

"If you leave don't come back and I mean it. Not tonight, not ever. It's over." Sara went out the door and closes it behind her. Tina stands in disbelief. A minute later Sara was knocking on the door. Tina opens the door.

"I thought you would see it my way." Sara snatches the blunt out of Tina's hand and sits on the couch. Tina sits on her lap and kisses her. Even though she is mad at her she gets up and fix her a drink. Tina wanted to play. She kept feeling on Sara's titties but Sara was not in the mood. Tina gives her a bag of dope and goes to bed. Sara sits at the table until her dope was gone and then she turns in. She rubs on Tina's vagina. Now Tina wasn't in the mood to play. So they quietly lay beside one another until they went to sleep. November 19, 1998, and it was Sara's birthday. Linda threw her a little get together. Tina was out the closet now. She didn't care anymore. Everybody knew about her and Sara. She was in love with Sara. Sara was drunk and dancing with a guy. She was bending over and he was feeling all over her. Tina didn't like it. She snatches Sara by her arm and they get into an argument. Tina takes her home. It was already late so Linda ends the party. Tina and Sara were at home, still arguing. Sara hits Tina and calls her a bitch. Tina tells her to get out and go sleep at Linda's. Tina goes to Linda's house about twenty minutes later. Everyone was gone and Linda was still cleaning up.

"Where is Sara?"

"She's not here. Did you two get in a fight?"

"Yes. I got to find her." Tina left and got her keys and rushes in her car. She rode around for about an hour looking for Sara. Tina went back to Linda's to see if she had come back.

"No." Linda said. Tina sits in the chair with tears in her eyes.

Linda looks at her and asked, "You really love my sister don't you?"

"Yes," Tina said, as a tear rolls down her face. Tina left. Tina went back to Linda's the next morning to see if Sara was there. Still no sign of Sara. Linda still had not heard from her sister. Tina collects the little money Linda had made and drives over to Grandma Mable's house looking for Sara at the same time. Tina spends the entire day eating and watching TV. When she arrives home she stops by Linda's. She was now worried. Sara had not been tricking in a while and she usually came back after a fight. Sunday morning, Linda gets a knock at the front door. It was the police. She was scared. She hides her dope and then answers the door.

"Good morning ma'am. Do you have a sister name Sara?"

"Yes." Linda replies.

"We have reason to believe that Sara is dead. We need you to come down to the morgue to identify her body." Linda was in a daze. She did not know what to think. She got her next-door neighbor to watch her kids and then she races up to Tina's. After telling Tina what the police said they both break down crying.

"They are not sure yet. Please get dressed and ride with me to the morgue." When they get downtown to the morgue a man leads them into a room. Tina stays in the hallway. Then she hears a loud scream... it was Linda. The man takes Linda out the room. Tina clutches her and leads her out. When they get back home Linda calls family and friends. Now they were planning Sara's funeral. The next day, Tina and Linda hustle up money for the funeral. Business was slow but they sold what they could. Tina made a call to Big Daddy to see if he could loan her $500. She told him about Sara and he stops by and gives her the money. That Friday, Linda finished selling all the dope they had. The following Sunday they had Sara's funeral. She had a nice wake and funeral. A lot people showed their respects for Sara. Tina and Linda sat beside each other, holding one another tight. When the funeral was over they went back home. Tina was out of pocket and it was the 1st of the month and the bills had to be paid. Later that evening, she calls Big Daddy and tells him she needs at least a quarter to get back on and that she will pay him back as soon as she made the money.

"What can you do for me?" Big Daddy questioned.

"Bring me the dope and I will make it worth your while." Big Daddy was 42-years old and he loved younger women. He really wanted Tina. That night he shows up and gives her the quarter. Tina takes him to her bedroom and did what she does best. She didn't enjoy it at all but she had to pay her bills. It took her a few times flipping quarters, but she got back up to a half of ounce. A couple of weeks later she was able to pay Big Daddy his $1500 back. Things were back to normal and Tina and Linda were still doing their thing. Tina was high and decides to go to the club. It was jammed packed as usual. She orders her usual drink and chicken wings. A guy hollers at her and they share laughs and drink the entire night.

"Well I have to go." Tina said.

"Can I go with you?"

"Yes." Tina answers.

He follows her home in his Mercedes Benz. She knew he was a big balla, but she knew she was not ready for a real relationship either. It had been a while since she felt a penis inside of her and all she wanted to do was fuck. They engage in some small talk for about 20 minutes, until Tina got tired of the chitchat.

"Excuse me for a minute." She said.

She goes into her room and comes back with her little short gown on. She went over to the guy and sits on his lap. She starts kissing him as he runs his hands up her thighs towards her vagina.

"Baby girl, I'm married."

"No problem. I just want to borrow you for tonight," Tina said as she leads him to the bedroom. They get naked and he sticks his penis inside of her. He didn't give Tina any foreplay. And at this moment Tina could care less. It felt so good to have a man between her legs. When she climaxes, she spreads her legs wide and screams with ecstasy.

"Fuck me!" When she finished her orgasm, she wraps her legs around his waist and rolls her ass. He was all right; she ponders to herself. About 30 minutes later they both climax and then he gets dressed and leaves. She didn't care. She got what she wanted and she knew she did not want to see him again. When she gets up to Linda's the next morning to collect, she was still in the bed with a hangover. Tina cooks breakfast for her and the kids. They fellowship at the table and reminisce about some of the crazy things Sara would say or do.

"I miss that girl." Tina said.

"I do too." Linda added.

Chapter 15

It's January 4, 1999, Ice Man's lawyer got him a plea of 15 years. He was sent to Central Prison in Raleigh NC. Sheila hated that for her son but she knew she had to be strong, so she could be there for him. Sheila and her son had a close relationship. It was his first year playing football for PAL North and he played basketball for The Boys & Girls Club. He was pretty good. One day while Sheila was gassing up her car she met a guy named Drew. He's 34-years old and has his own sheet rock business and he was tall, dark and handsome. They talk for a minute and then she gives him her number, gets in her car and drives off. She had not seen or heard from Tina in while. She wanted to stop by her house but her pride got in the way. She needed someone to talk to. Tina was always that 'go to' person. Friday night, Sheila got her mother to babysit. She gets dressed and goes to The Maze. She hadn't been out in a while and she needed some alone time to herself. When she gets there she dances and talks with a few people she knew. It wasn't the same because she was not high. Plus, B-Money, Tina and Ice-Man were not there. She left and rides by Tina's apartment to see if she was there. She didn't see Tina's car so she left. Someone in the club told Sheila about Tina and Sara.

Tina went to see Grandma Mable that Saturday evening. On her way she stops at McDonald's to get a bite to eat.

When she arrives at Grandma Mable's, she was happy as usual to see her.

"You look different." said Grandma Mable. Tina had put on a little weight since Sara had died. She was looking good, while still maintaining her habit. Tina spent the rest of the evening with Grandma. She told Tina that her sugar was getting worse. Tina went outside to blaze a blunt. It was chilly and windy out, so she hurried back in. Grandma Mable knew Tina was smoking weed. But she still hid it like she was a teenager. She always respected her grandmother. When she got back in, the 8'oclock movie was about to come on. She chills and watches the movie. When Tina returns home the jump out van was in front of Linda's apartment. She sits outside on the other end of the parking lot. Then the police bring Linda out in handcuffs. They put her in the backseat of the police car and had another car for her kids. Later, Linda gets in touch with Tina. She tells her that her bond is $25,000 and she wanted to know if she could come and get her out. Tina said she would be there in the morning to get her out. The next morning Tina had to pawn all of her jewelry to put with the little money she had to bail Linda out of jail. She was not about to sleep with Big Daddy's nasty ass again. But she knew she had to get Linda out of jail. They had become close, like sisters. The next day Linda told Tina that she was through with selling drugs. Her kids were now in the custody of social services. She has court date next week and since she didn't have any priors, the drug charge sentenced her to a drug program and on completion she would get her kids back. She contacts her uncle and had him to put her things in his attic and then she went to

Black Mountain for treatment. Tina felt alone. She was out of pocket again. She spent the whole week looking for a job but no one was hiring. She was getting frustrated because some days she wanted to get high but she couldn't. Tina ran into a girl from back in the day. Her name was Sandy. Sandy was 29 and had the perfect body. They stood outside of Burger King talking. Tina had just filled out an application. Sandy told her she could get her a job at Mrs. Kitty Kats.

"What's that?" Tina asked.

"It's a strip club." Tina got the address from Sandy and later that evening she checks it out. She has conversation with a man named Jimmy. He hires her on the spot and lets her know to be ready for work at 9:00 PM. Tina's first night was crazy. Guys were waving their money at her and she loved it. When she got off she thanked Sandy for helping her out. On the way home she rides through the Blvd. While riding she sees Tonya and picks her up.

"Do you know where I can get something to smoke?" Tina had made $115 in tips. She took her to Lil Rob's. He sold nothing but 20's. Tina gave her $60 to get three. She had to save some of her money to pay on her phone bill. They went back to Tina's place and had a few hits. Then Tonya had to use the bathroom. When she got up Tina looks at Tonya's shape. She wasn't Tina's type. Tonya was undesirably, dark skin and ugly. She was also on the heavy side. When they finished getting high, Tina let Tonya chill for about thirty minutes before she said she was ready to go to bed.

"Can you give me a ride back to the Blvd?"

"Yes." Tina said. When Tina dropped Tonya off, she swung by Lil Rob's and got her another twenty and went home. The next morning, she borrowed $60 from Grandma Mable to pay her phone and water bill. When she got paid Tina thought about getting a package but she was scared. The spot where she lived was still hot. So she kept going to Lil Rob. She became a regular. And he was trying to hit the vagina. Tina went to work on Monday and business was slow, but she made a few bucks off of tips. When she got off of work she went to Lil Rob's to purchase $40 worth. She went home and realized she spent all she had and Tina was feening bad. The dope she had was good and she wanted some more. Five in the morning she rides back over to Lil Rob's place. He was standing behind a tree and came out when he sees her car pull up.

"Whatcha need baby girl?"

"Let me get a twenty until tomorrow. You know I will pay you back." Tina said.

"I don't do the credit thing. But I will look out for you if you lick."

"Okay. Get in." They go to Tina's apartment. Lil Rob gives her the dope and she smokes a little piece. She takes her clothes off after the last hit and walks over to him and takes his penis out. He was sitting on the couch, so she bends down on her knees between his legs. His penis was so big. When she starts sucking it she knew he was going to hurt her because she hadn't had sex in a while. He pulls his pants off and lays her on the couch. He had to force his penis inside of her tight vagina because she kept moving. Once he got it all in, she let out a loud scream. While pushing him back off of her, he lifts her legs high in the air and begin to beat her vagina like he was going crazy. Tina could not move. Lil Rob had her penned down. Then she found a way to push him up off of her.

"You better take it easy or you ain't getting no more." She said. He snatches her up and tells her to get in the bed. They go into the bedroom and he lays her down and then puts his monster of a penis back inside of her. He put his hand under her shoulder locking her in place so she can't move or throw him off again. He starts beating her vagina as hard as he can. By this time, Tina was crying and asking him to please take it easy. She repeats it over and over again. But he keeps on fucking her. After 40 minutes of beating her vagina lips sideways he tells her to get up and turn around.

"No!" Tina said. Lil Rob was furious.

"Bitch you smoked my dope! Turn your ass around." When he sticks his penis in her from behind Tina could not do anything but cry. Lil Rob climaxed inside of Tina 15 minutes later.

"Take me back to the spot." He said after he finished beating her vagina to death. Tina drops him off and says he would never get anymore vagina from her again. He sticks up his middle finger as she pulls off.

Tina went back home to finish smoking her dope. She rests all day before work. When she gets to work her and Sandy had a talk.

"Is everything alright?" Sandy inquired.

"Yeah." Tina replied. Sandy was working the stage while Tina danced on the floor giving lap dances. Some guy asked her if he could holler at her after work. Tina declines the offer.

Chapter 16

Two months had gone by and Linda was back home from living with her uncle. His wife had died and she was staying in a big three-bedroom house. Her first week home she had to meet with her social worker. He set up a date for her to visit with her kids. She also has to take a drug test twice a month. Linda was happy about that. Two days later she was able to see her kids and they were very happy to see her. She told them about her new life and how she was going to get them back, as long as she stayed clean from drugs. She was able to spend 2 hours with the kids. She told them she would be back next week to see them and every week after that. Linda got involved with Narcotics Anonymous and attends support group meetings. She got her a sponsor and three weeks later she was hired at Pizza Hut. Her uncle truly enjoyed Linda's company. While Linda was living there, her 68-years old uncle didn't have to cook for himself. He allowed Linda to drive his car to her meetings and to work. Linda was enjoying her new life. After being in fellowship for two months a guy named Tim asked her out on a date. Tim had been clean for 3 years. Linda felt there was no harm in going out with him. Linda was still in compliance with her orders in successfully passing her drug tests and visiting her kids every week. About 3 months later her worker gave her list of section-8 houses. She took the list home and looked it over. She called Tim to tell him the good news. Tim had his own apartment and he knew the feeling she was expressing about her accomplishments. It was Friday night and Linda asked Tim if she could come over after the meeting. He agrees. Linda was finally ready to let the wall down that she had up for many years. She had been so afraid to get into a relationship. But Tim made her feel like he was the one. At the meeting that evening, Linda shared her proud moment. She met Tim at his place and they talk for a while before Linda shared.

"I haven't slept with a man in a while."

He laughed as he replied, "Stop playing."

"No I'm for real Tim."

"That thing got spider webs on it." Tim said jokingly.

"No silly. I have been in abusive relationships and hurt by every man that I was involved with."

"I understand if you need more time. Take your time," Tim said with all seriousness.

"No." She said, as she grabs him by the hand and pulls him on top of her. They begin to share a kiss. Tim picks her up off the couch and takes her to his bedroom. They kiss and touch one another's faces for a minute. Tim unbuttons her pants and she pulls them off. They were now both naked. Tim kisses her neck softly as he gently plays in her vagina. Getting it loose and wet as he sucks on her titties. Linda could not hold her composure any longer. She was so horny she was about to explode. She pulls him on top of her and spreads her legs as she pulls his penis towards her vagina and eases it inside of her.

"Damn!" She hollers. She forgot how good sex was. She bust on him in ten minutes and kept on moaning and rolling her ass. He wanted her to ride him.

"I'm not ready for all of that." Linda said. Her sex was so good to Tim. He had not slept with anyone since he had broken up with Debbie four months ago. When he came inside of her, Linda said, "Thank you."

He replied, "No thank you." Linda stayed the night cuddled up with Tim. The next morning, he takes her shopping and bought her some clothes. Tim was a local truck driver. He liked it because he was able to work close to home and Linda loved it too. A couple months went by and Linda had finally gotten her apartment. Tim helped her furnish the apartment. Her uncle gave her his car and she got a job at Pic and Pay Warehouse, working first shift. Her social worker came out for a home visit and he loved how nice Linda had the apartment set up. Two weeks later her kids came home. Linda felt like God had blessed her. She felt the only way to repay him was to faithfully continue going to her meetings. After her kids were settled, a couple of days later she felt it was time to introduce them to Tim. Her son was 16 and her daughter was 14. Tim spent the day getting to know the kids. They all ate dinner together and afterwards he and Linda watched a movie. Ricco and Shana went outside to check out their new neighborhood. As Linda sits next to Tim she gives him a kiss and said, "Thank you for being here for me. I am happier than I've ever been before in my life." It was late, so Tim says he would call her when he gets home. He leaves and when Linda was getting ready for bed she calls her kids in the room where she is.

What do you two think about Tim?"

"He is cool." They both said.

"And nice."

"I hope he has money I need new clothes." Shana said. Then they laugh. Meanwhile, Sheila had received a letter from Ice Man. He had been shipped off to Warren Correctional Institute, to a medium custody facility. He said it wasn't all that bad. But he missed having his own room. He wrote how he had changed his life and was going to church and reading the bible. He didn't sleep well at night because of the disturbing thoughts of him killing the little boy would not get out of his head. He told her that he even wrote the little boy's parents a letter sharing his sympathy and apologized for what he had done. He told them in the letter if he could switch places with the little boy that he would. He understands that there is nothing he or anyone can do to bring him back. He asked them to forgive him for the mistakes he had made and that he hoped that they could forgive him as well. Two weeks later he received a letter from the little boy's mother. In the letter the mother said that she was a Christian woman and that she forgives him and that God was the only way out. He told Sheila he wished he could go back and do things differently. The letter was touching to Sheila that she wrote him back. Before she took out her pen and paper she sat on the couch and began thinking back on the good times they had coming up in school and beyond. She even thought about Tina. Then her phone rings, it's Drew.

"Hey baby."

"Hello," She replied speaking in a dry tone.

"Is everything okay?"

"Yes." She replied. They talk for a few minutes and she tells him she had to call him back later. When she hangs up she asked her son for pen and paper. She tells him to write his father also. Then she pens this letter to Ice Man.

Dear Ice-Man,

I think about you a lot. Especially, how we first met and got together. You were crazy. But you were and still are a good person. We all make mistakes. So who am I to judge? I am not perfect and I will never be. So if God can forgive me so can I. I don't know why you slept with Tina. But in my heart I forgive the both of you. I miss how we all used to hang out. I wish I could hold you in my arms and kiss you. I can't promise you that I will wait 15 years. You know that is a long time. But I will always be your friend and I will always love you forever. I will bring our son to see you as soon as possible. I don't want him growing up thinking that his father is a bad man. Because I know you are not and God does too. So you take care of #1.

Love you,

Sheila

She cries herself to sleep after writing the letter. When she wakes up it was 8:30 PM. She fixes her a bite to eat and then remembers she forgot to call Drew back. They talk for a while until she had to get ready for bed. She had work the next morning. At the end of the week Drew took Sheila out to eat and bowling. She loved bowling. They had become very close. Even her son had taken a liking to him. He even mentioned taking the relationship a step further a time or two. But Sheila was not ready for a commitment. Drew was a great guy and she cares for him a lot. But she felt he was rushing things and she told him to slow down. Sheila enjoys working at Lance. And she loves the fact that her and her mother were building their relationship with one another.

Chapter 17

It's 2001 and Tina lost everything she owned from using drugs and living from pillow to post. She's always telling herself, one day she will get back on. She was walking down the street on the late night and a guy asked if she wanted to get high. She said, "Yes." He leads her to an empty house. When she gets through the backdoor he hits her upside the head knocking her to the floor. She was too dizzy to scream. She knew it would not have done any good.

"You better be quiet," he said as he pulls her clothes off. He rapes her for hours and leaves her laying there. She felt like she wanted to kill herself. But she just lays there balled up wanting to hit some dope. It wasn't long before the sun came up. She runs into some guys that had just coped two dimes. She smokes with them behind the store. One of the guys went back to the guy that was standing in front of the store and coped two more. Then him, Tina and his friend go to the boarding house where he and his friend live. His friend pours Tina a shot of Vodka. Then he smokes three bags with her.

Then he tells Tina, "You have to give up some head and vagina." She really didn't want to, but she didn't want to get beat up and raped again either. Tina asked for another drink and a hit of dope. They give her what she asked for, when she took off her shirt. While she was hitting a piece of dope, one of the guys rubs her titties. Now they all were naked. They lay Tina on her side, while one hits it from the back, the other sticks his penis in her mouth. This was her first time ever taking care of two men at the same time. Most of the time, Tina would not bust a nut because she would not enjoy whom she was having sex with. After a while, the guys switched on Tina. One of them sticks his penis in her ass. She really hated that. Then they put her out. She finally made it back to Mary's house where she's been staying. She did not have any clothes there but she washes up and changes into what she has. Mary lives with her boyfriend. Tina had to fuck and suck him too, when he got the chance. They asked Tina if she had any dope. She told them no, but she did. She told them goodnight and went to sleep. Two weeks had gone by and she was tired of sucking and fucking Mary's boyfriend in order to stay there without paying rent. Every time Mary would leave he expected something out of Tina or he threatened to put her out if she didn't do what he asked of her. A few weeks had passed and Tina was standing outside the store when a man picks her up. She felt his penis and asked him if he wanted to buy some vagina. He drove around the back.

"You are under arrest."

He showed her his badge and locks her up. She stays in jail for 30 days before she's released. She hadn't seen Grandma Mable in a while, so she went straight there.

"Grandma, can I stay here for a while?"

"Yes." Grandma Mable replied. She knew Tina was a drug addict. But that was her granddaughter and she loved Tina. One morning Grandma Mable went to cash her disability check, while Tina turned tricks for favors. Tina returns back home shell as hell. That was her first hit since she got out of jail and she was back out the door, feening for some more dope. She went back to the store where the young guys were standing that sold her the first hit. It was three of them. They were tripping off of Suzie. She was another dope addict. When Tina walks up she ask one of the young guys for some credit. He didn't know her like that was his response. One of the guys told her that he would give her a dime piece for a freak show. Susie asked Tina if she was down with it. Tina said yes. They took the girls in a house and gave them dimes. The three guys were in their early 20's. They just wanted to watch and trip off of ladies. They told them to get naked and lie in the living room floor and do the 69. The girls laid on their sides, one facing up and the other down. They both gap their legs open and start licking and sucking on one another's vaginas. The guys had them stick two fingers inside of each other and they did. They did this for about ten minutes. One of the guys tells them it was enough because it was time for his sister to come home. The girls left and went to Mable's to smoke their dope.

After they got high Tina asked Suzie, "Where do you hang out at?"

"Over on 2nd Street."

"Do a lot of guys spend money over there?"

"Yes." Suzie replied Suzie went on her way. Tina fell back for a while. It wasn't long before Grandma Mable would be coming home from paying a few bills. When she got in, Tina was sleep, so she prepares dinner. About 7:00 PM Grandma Mable gets in the shower and Tina goes in Grandma Mabel's room and takes her money out of her pocketbook. Then she eases out the door. When Grandma Mable gets out of the shower she notices that Tina was gone. When she goes to her room to get dressed, she finds her pocket book wide open. She looks inside and her money was gone. She knew Tina was an addict but she never would have thought she would steal from her. All Grandma Mable could do was cry. She looks out the door and Tina was nowhere to be found. Tina had stolen $320 from Grandma Mable. Tina remembers Big Daddy's number and she tries giving him a call but his number had been changed. She went over to 2nd Street and there is where she finds Suzie, the girl from earlier. She showed Tina where she could get some weight and they went and bought some sandwich bags. It was time for Tina to get back on. Suzie took Tina to a friend's house by the name of Sharon. Sharon was a smoker also and she had gotten her check today to. Tina went back to selling dope. Sharon allowed Tina to bag up her dope and Tina gave her a twenty piece of shake. Tina took one hit while Sharon and Suzie smoked what they had. Sharon had a clean little house with two bedrooms. Tina had already plotted in her mind and she waited until after Sharon bought a few more dimes before she popped the question.

"Sharon I have nowhere to stay right now. Can I stay with you for a few days?"

"Yes." Sharon said. The next morning, while Grandma Mabel was at the doctor, Tina snuck over and grab some clothes and left. When she got back Suzie was there. She gave her a dime and told her to let everyone know that she was holding. Then she went out on the side of Sharon's house near the woods and hid her dope. She bagged up $620 worth of dimes, that she cut up out of a quarter she bought for $300. That morning, Suzie was bringing in the customers. She even made $40 for sucking and fucking two guys in the woods. When she came out the woods, Tina was joking with her.

"Make that money girl. Don't let that money make you."

"Shut up." Suzie said. "Give me four." About 4:00 that afternoon Tina takes a break. She goes in and gives Sharon $20 and Sharon tells her to give her two dimes instead. A little later on Tina went back out. It was slow. Around 11:00 PM Tina hid her dope back in the woods. She kept five bags on her just in case Suzie came back. About midnight there was no Suzie. So Tina smoked two bags with Sharon and went off to sleep. The next morning Tina went to the store and bought some breakfast and a six-pack of Budweiser. She went back home to cook and eat and then the customers started coming. Now she had enough money to re-up. She left Sharon with the dope she had and went on 6th Street. Sharon didn't care about Tina selling but she did not want anyone smoking in her house, except for Suzie and Tina. When Tina got to 6th Street she looked for Chuck. He was the guy Suzie turned her on to. He was married but he kept his wife at his other house across town. He sold his dope out of a junkie's house. When she went in she asked him for another quarter. He went out back and came back in and called her to come in another room.

After he sold her the dope he asks, "Do you have a man?"

"No." she replied.

"Here is my number. Stay in touch." Chuck drives a 92 SUV and made good money selling nothing but halves and quarters. Tina gets back to Sharon's so she can bag up her dope. Within a months' time Tina was back on. She was looking like the old Tina again. She bought new clothes and a cellphone and had moved up from buying quarters to halves. She was still smoking a little, but she was about her money. Tina always had a business mindset when it came to getting paid in the dope game. Now all she needed was the right spot to hustle out of and she found it. Suzie ended up finding her a Sugar Daddy to take care of her. He stayed around the corner from Sharon. He was 67 years old. The only thing she did was suck his penis and give him a little bit of vagina. Tina asked Suzie one day if he could still get it up. She told her it would stand up like a young boy when he takes Viagra. He receives a retirement and disability check, so Suzie stays up under him during the first of the month.

Chapter 18

Tina had been staying with Sharon for 3 months now. Her little spot was booming. They ate good, smoked well and drank even better. Every now and then Sharon would let her friend guy come and hit her vagina. Tina had gone out with Chuck but he had not hit it yet. One night he took Tina out. He told her he had to go buy some dope. She rode with him. His friend had an enormous house with a lot of yard. Chuck parks on the side of the house by some trees. When he gets his dope he tells his homeboy that he has a girl in the jeep, and that he could only holler at him for a minute. Once he returns to his jeep, he and Tina engaged in conversation. He starts up the jeep and turns the air on. Chuck reaches over and gives Tina a kiss. She puts her hands around his neck and kisses him back. He rubs her vagina through her tights. He pulls her to the backseat and takes her clothes off. Then he removes his. She was horny. He sucks on her titties as he lays her down. She asked him to turn the air up a little. It was in the month of May and it was a tad bit warm outside. He pulls her head down towards his penis and she starts sucking it gently, pulling it up and down in her mouth. He couldn't believe how good she sucked his penis. Tina blew his mind as she deep throated his penis. Tina knew what she was doing. She was trying to turn Chuck out. She told him to lay on his back and stick his penis in her tight vagina as she rides it backwards. It felt so good to her because again she had not had any in a while.

Chuck tells her how good it is and she bounces up and down on his penis real fast screaming, "Fuck me!"

"Get up." Chuck said. He didn't want any cum on his seats so he reaches back and grabs a towel. He places it on the seat and she sits her ass cheeks on the towel. He put one of her legs over his shoulder and the other across the seat. Then he sticks his penis back inside of her, beating her vagina like crazy. Tina was moaning trying hard not to holler. But it felt so good to her and even better to Chuck because he nutted inside of her. He took her back to Sharon's house. Tina kind of figured Chuck had a woman but she was playing him for dope. When she got in she was not thinking about making money for the rest of the night. She had been fucked well and she wanted to get high. Her and Sharon get high and then Suzie pops up. She didn't stay long. She had to get back to her old man. The next day Tina gets a call from Chuck.

"Can we get together later?"

"I will give you a call back later and let you know." she replied. Tina downs her Budweiser and smokes a blunt with Sharon. It was hot; Tina went outside and sits in a chair under the tree. She was trying to make her some money. Her past started racing through her head. She thought about B-Money, Sheila, Ice Man, Sara and even thought about when she was raped. Her thoughts were interrupted when a guy came up wanting five dimes. Then a girl walks up wanting two. After the sun went down she went in and talked with Sharon for a while. She went back out around 9:00 PM. People were coming back to back. They were telling Tina how good her dope was. She called Chuck and told him she was going to chill for the night. The following morning, Tina wrote her Grandma Mable a letter telling her how sorry she was for stealing her money. She put $200 in the envelope, but she didn't put a return address on it. She didn't want Grandma Mable to know where she was staying. Tina walks to the store. It was the first of the month and Tina had $500. She called Chuck and told him she needed a half. He told her he would be there in a few. When he pulls up, Tina hops in. It was feeling good in his jeep. Tina kisses him and he gives her the dope.

"What's up with the short ass skirt?" he asked.

She laughed, "Nothing."

"I'm a little jealous." He tells Tina.

"Don't be out here selling dope in no damn skirt." She looks at him as he said,

"Now let me see dem panties." She turns towards him and gap her legs open. He reaches over and feels her vagina asking her, "Can I get some tonight?"

"No. I need to make some money and it's plenty coming through." Chuck left and she went in and bags up her dope. She smokes a little piece and gives Sharon the shake. Then goes outside to hide her package. A police rode by, but he didn't pay Tina sitting in the chair any attention. Tina got nervous being out there all alone. Two hours had gone by and no one had come through so she went in. Sharon was in her room smoking so Tina sat on the couch. She knew she had to fuck Chuck during the week because she was caught up in the game again. Tina felt like there was nothing like fucking a nigga who can keep her on. She loves money and she loves getting high. About 10:00 that night Suzie came by. She bought five dimes and smoked them with Sharon. Tina didn't want to get too high. She wanted to stay focused. When Suzie got through smoking and her high came down, she tells Tina she had a pistol for sale. The old man she was in love with had three pistols and two shotguns in the house. She wanted to sell it her the .32 for three dimes. Tina told her to go get it. When Suzie got back with the gun it was already loaded. She gave Suzie the dope and smoked a dime with Sharon before she left. Tina sat by the window watching for customers at 1:35 in the morning. A few came through and she went out to serve them. She told them to get all they needed because she was not coming back out. She made a quick $40 and went back inside. The next morning a man knocks on the door. She let him know not to knock on the door if he didn't see her in the yard. She went outside and sold him some dope. She went in to fix some breakfast and then Chuck calls.

"What's up?" He said.

"Nothing." Tina replied.

"You want to go for a ride?"

"Yeah." He pulls up twenty minutes later. She gets in and they ride off towards the highway. They stop by a store and get a six-pack of Budweiser. Then he takes Tina to the lake. They talk and get high. He steps out the car to make a phone call.

"Hey David. What's up? Hey man I need to use the crib. I'm on the way out now."

"I will leave the door unlock for you." Chuck and David were boys. David had blown up off the dope him and Strawberry had hit B-Money up for years back. Chuck got back in the car and took Tina to David's house. He fucks her good for two hours. They wash off and he takes her back home.

When she gets ready to get out she asked him, "Where do you live?"

"I can't tell you that."

"Why? Do you have a woman?"

"Something like that." Chuck replied. She rolls her eyes at him and he grabs her by the arm and said, "I still love you baby girl."

"Whatever," she said and got out the jeep.

What Chuck really loved was how Tina threw that vagina on him. She was sitting in the yard under the tree, when a guy came up to buy some dope. Tina remembered his face from Linda's house back in the day. He bought two dimes.

"What is your name?" she asked.

"Frank."

"I remember you from Linda's house back in the day."

"I remember you too."

"Can you watch my back while I sell my dope? I will give you more dope at the end of the night." He was down with it.

"Yes, but I need to hit one first." She told him to go in the woods while she went inside and got her pistol. She sticks it in her pocket and pulls her shirt down over it. It was hot as hell in the middle of June. Tina had made $280 by midnight. She was ready to go in and Frank could not wait to smoke. She gave him three dimes and he was satisfied. When he left she put her dope in another hiding spot. Then she went in and fire up one with Sharon. Tina had a lot on her mind. She could not sleep. She was missing her Grandma Mabel. She lays back down. The next morning, she made up her mind to go see her Grandma Mabel. Frank came walking up at 10:00 AM with a Colt 45 in hand.

"Hey Tina."

"Hey Frank." They sit in the yard under the tree and talk.

"Tina can I get a dime to get the hanks off of me?" She gives him one. She hid her dope around the back. She lets Frank know that from now on she was selling out the back while he watched the front. Around 4:00 she told Frank she had to go make a run. She didn't stay that far from Grandma Mable, maybe about 15 minutes walking distance.

"I will be back about 7:00. Here is my cell number to call me just in case I am not back yet." It was hot outside but Tina strikes out walking. When she arrives she is tired from that walk in the heat. It took her exactly 20 minutes to get to Grandma Mable's house.

When she knocks on the door Grandma Mable hollers, "Who is it?"

"Tina." Mable opens the door and gives Tina a hug. Tina conveys to Grandma how sorry she is for all the pain she has caused her. They sit and talk for a while and then Tina tells Mable she has to go. She reaches in her pocket and hands Grandma Mable $150 but she would not take it.

"Keep it. You might need it." Tina threw the money on the coffee table and walk out. When she gets halfway back Frank calls and she lets him know that she was coming down Pecan Avenue on her way back. As soon as she arrives, Frank was waiting. She went in to get her pistol, drink some water and returns to talk to Frank. They talk about life and all of the things they had been through. Frank tells Tina he lives with his mother and he has three kids who live with their mother and that he was single. He told her he and his baby mama were cool and when he was working he gave her money. Frank loved beer. He was sipping on a 40-ounce Colt 45 when a customer walks up. It was a woman, jumping out the car with a white man.

Tina goes around the corner and tells her, "Never get out in front of the house." And sold her twelve dimes for $100. The girl ran out the yard and jumps back in the car. Tina sits back down and her and Frank pick back up with their conversation. Before they knew it, three more people came up wanting dope. About thirty minutes later Tina had Frank to hold her pistol. She trusted him for some reason. She went inside to count her money. She had $510 and she was ready to get another half from Chuck. But she wasn't ready to call him. She gave Sharon the money to hold for her. She went back outside and less than an hour later it was dark. She retrieves her package and she still had 29 dimes left.

She tells Frank, "At 11:00, I'm closing shop." At that moment a girl and a guy walk up. They had a gold rope necklace and they wanted five dimes for it. Tina bought it from them. When 10:45 hit she gets her pistol from Frank and gives him five dimes. Frank was ready to go find him a trick. When Tina got in she felt funny. She had already missed her period. Early the next morning she went to the store and bought a home pregnancy test. When she got back and took the test, Tina was pregnant. She called a cab and went to the abortion clinic. They made her an appointment and she left. When she got back she did not tell anyone. Tina wanted kids but she felt like it was not the right time, especially with Chuck. He was very demanding. He told Tina not to wear tight shorts up her ass and she dressed too sexy. She still had her tight body. She was 5'8, 120 pounds with nice little titties and a firm ass. She was wearing 138 but she lost a lot of weight from smoking crack. A week later Tina made her appointment. That evening when she got back she chilled. She gave Frank the dope for him to sell for her.

Chapter 19

It was the 4th of July 2002. Tina told Frank she was chilling because she was going to a cookout. She gave him two dimes and $5 on GP. Then he left. She went in to get dressed. Chuck pulls up about 2:00 in a small car. She got in and gives him a kiss.

"Whose car?" She asked.

"Mine." He said as they ride off. When they arrive at David's house they walk around back where everyone is. Chuck introduces her to some of the guest at the cookout.

"What do you want to drink?" Chuck asked Tina.

"A Gin and juice." She looks around and Sandy was standing behind her. They give each other a hug. Then they talked about the past. Chuck brought her a drink and asked her where she knew Sandy from. She told him that they had gone to school together. Sandy told Tina she was no longer dancing at the club, how she met David at the club and he wines and dines her, and now they are engaged. She points David out to her.

He was standing at the grill cooking. After a while David hollers, "The food is done." Everyone rushes to the table and grab a plate and fix their food. When Tina looks at David she knew she remembered him from somewhere.

They had BBQ ribs, burgers, hotdogs, steaks, and BBQ chicken, corn on the cob, cole slaw, and fried fish, baked beans and more. It reminded her of the last cookout she went to at Sheila's house years ago. After she ate she had a few drinks and a couple of beers. She had to pee so David shows her where the restroom is.

"Do you remember me?"

"No." Tina said.

"I picked you up on the Blvd a while back. You look good. Don't worry I won't tell Chuck." She uses the bathroom and goes back outside. The cookout died down around 8:15 PM.

"Are you ready to go?" Chuck asked Tina.

"Yes." she replied. Before they left she thanked David for not saying anything to Chuck.

When they pull out the driveway he asked Tina, "Do you want to go to the hotel with me?"

"Yes." When they get inside the room they took off all their clothes. Tina lays across the bed on her stomach. She was feeling nice and Chuck was too. He gives her a soothing massage, running his hands up and down her back and around her ass cheeks. He spreads her legs and plays with her clit. He kisses her neck and sticks two fingers in her vagina. She hunches her ass up a little so he could stick his fingers all the way in. Her vagina was so juicy. He turns her over on her back and pecks her, as he rubs the hairs on her vagina. He caresses her small titties while sucking both of them. Tina's vagina was throbbing as if it she was about to cum. She sits up and positions his penis inside her mouth and moves her head up and down fast as she deep throats him. All he could do is grab the back of her head and push it down, trying to see how much she can take in her mouth.

"Damn!" He said. Then his phone rings. She still has his penis in her mouth. She was horny as hell.

"It might be important." He said. It was his wife. He told her he would be home shortly. Tina didn't like that response at all.

When he disconnects the call Tina said, "I don't like any nigga fucking me and leaving. Can you stay the night?"

"I will be back. Let me finish." And she did. He got between her thighs and inserts his penis back inside of her. She rolls her ass as she moans out of control. He places her in the buck and her moans grew louder.

"Fuck me Chuck!" Tina shouts. "Fuck me, fuck me, fuck me!" Tina turns over and gets on her knees and allows Chuck to slide himself in from the back. No matter how many times it had been beat, Tina knew her vagina was good. It always got back tight. She yells and moans telling Chuck not to stop. She busts two nuts in thirty minutes. Now her vagina was real wet. Chuck loved fucking Tina. Then it was his turn to bust a nut. She lays on her back as he shakes it off, she pulls him for more. Tina was still horny.

Chuck washes up and tells her, "Chill Tina. I told you I would be back." Tina got up and took a shower. After she got out of the shower she said, Fuck him. She calls her a cab and goes home. When she gets in, she rolls a blunt and after smoking she goes to find Frank.

Chuck calls. "Where are you?"

"I came home." Chuck is now upset and hangs up the phone.

While Tina and Frank were in front of Sharon's house, Chuck rides pass. He didn't stop because Frank was with Tina. About 11:30 Tina lets Frank know that she was going in around 1:00 AM. A few people were coming and there were others out popping firecrackers. Tina went inside and got her pistol and gave it to Frank. Chuck rides back up the street and Tina catches a glimpse of him and starts laughing.

"What was up with that?" Frank asked.

"He's my friend."

"Well I hope your friend ain't jealous and try to come back and shoot me."

"Shoot him back. What you got the pistol for if you scared to use it? Besides I wouldn't let that happen."

Tina made $90 and she gave Frank two bags. Tina went in and called Chuck. "I need a half and I only have $450."

"Why are you always short?" Chuck asked.

"I help pay bills and I help my Grandma out." Then she snapped. "Oh and you fucking me. Does that not count for something?"

Chuck laughed and said, "You can get it now if you go back to the room with me."

"Yes." Tina said. He picks her up.

"Do you still have the key?"

"Yes" Tina answered. When they got back Chuck did not waste any time getting naked. He even helped Tina take her clothes off. He kisses her and sticks his penis right inside of her. He was not into foreplay. He put her legs on his shoulders and went in deep. Tina was moaning real loud. He hits her walls and she starts squirming. She had squirmed all the way to the top of the bed. Her head was pressed against the headboard. Her vagina was so moist it was talking back to Chuck. Tina lay motionless as Chuck beat her vagina with a continuous thrust. Tina pushes him up off of her.

"Are you okay?" Chuck asked.

"Yes." Tina replied. Tina rolls over on top of Chuck and sticks his penis inside of her. She rolls slowly as he gets all of him inside of her. When her nut announces its presence, she starts screaming and bouncing up and down on his penis. As she nuts, Chuck flips her over and begins beating her vagina hard until he ejaculates inside of her. She didn't care now. Tina was on the pill. She lay there holding Chuck tight with her legs spread wide with her eyes closed.

"Tina you have some good sex girl."

"I know." Chuck was not the one that would stay out all night. But he did. About an hour later he fucks her again. He couldn't get enough. The next morning, he drops her off at home. Tina bags up her dope and gives Frank some to sell. She had to go see her Grandma Mable.

Grandma Mable was resting. She wasn't feeling well. So Tina stayed the whole day to keep an eye on her. When she got home Frank had sold $250 worth of dope for her. She had left him with $300 worth.

"Keep the last five. Tina told Frank. I'm calling it a night and Tina went inside. All she wanted to do was get high and she didn't want to be bothered. Tina gave Sharon a bag and then she went in her room to get high and went to bed. She couldn't control her habit at times. Sometimes she smoked all night long.

Chapter 20

A week later, Frank told Tina that he wanted to start selling the bags that she was giving him and that he was trying to slow down on getting high. They sold dope all that day. At the end of the night Tina gave him one bag and told him to come get $40 from her in the morning and go buy something for himself. The next morning, Frank did just that. When he got back he had a fresh haircut and a shave.

"Stay like that." Tina said to Frank. The next two weeks Frank bought him some clothes and shoes. He was fixing himself up and Tina kind of liked it. Tina and Frank had got closer over the past 6 month. Chuck wasn't feeling that. Tina told him that Frank just watched her back while she sells her dope. It had gotten to the point that Tina was leaving her dope and pistol with Frank. Frank was feeling Tina. But he didn't want her to know. It was November 19, 2002, the weather was neither warm nor cold. Tina had left to spend her Sunday with Grandma Mable. Chuck didn't have any dope, so he chilled.

Frank called Tina a little after 4PM, "What's up Tina?"

"Nothing much. I'm chilling with my Grandma."

"What time are you coming home?" He asked.

"About 6." She said.

"I got a pint of gin and juice for us. You know today is my birthday."

"Oh yeah, I forgot." When Tina got home, Frank came shortly after. Sharon was now okay with him coming inside of her house because he sold dope for Tina. However, she still would not allow him to smoke crack in her house. Tina had a six-pack of Budweiser in the fridge and Frank had the Gin. It was the night before Thanksgiving and Tina asked Frank to come around back with her.

"Do you have a stem on you." Tina asked.

"No." Frank replied. Tina went inside and came back out. They relaxed on the porch in the dark. Tina told Frank she smoked every now and then. She took a dime and gave him half of it. She told him not to say anything to anyone about her smoking. After they finished smoking, she took Sharon her stem back and fixed her and Frank a shot of Gin. They chilled back in the yard and up walks a white guy they never seen before. He had a fifty-dollar bill. They told him they didn't sell dope. So he left. One of Tina's regular customers came back for the white guy and told them that he was cool. Tina told him, when the white guy wants something, that he is to come for him. People started coming back to back. Tina told Frank to watch her back carefully as she sold the dope. A police car rode by but he didn't pay them any attention. Tina then started having the customers to come around back. After she made a sell, she would send them through a path in the woods that would bring them out on the next street. At the end of the night she gave Frank two bags. He knew that she would have his money in the morning.

"Would you like to smoke one of my bags with me?"

"No." Tina said. Then Frank left. It was Thanksgiving morning and Tina went to spend the day with Grandma Mable. Grandma Mable was doing fine. She had some family members to stop by to see her. Tina called Chuck but he was stuck with his wife and family. Tina got home around 2 AM. An hour later Frank shows up. He invites her to his house. His mother was gone out of town for a few days. Tina did not have anything else to do so she went. They ate some food that Frank's mother had prepared before she left. After eating, Frank pulls out a 5th of Gin. He knew Tina loved Gin. Tina fires up a blunt and they get high. It was late in the evening and the two were laughing and playing. Tina was feeling good. She rests across Frank's bed and states that she is cold. Frank turns up the heat and positions himself in the bed beside Tina. Frank kisses Tina and she kisses him back. He unbuttons her jeans and rubs her vagina. Frank takes off his clothes and sensually removes Tina's clothes and slides under the covers. Frank had a nice size penis and it felt good to Tina. She only allowed him to hit her one way and that was on top. Tina knew she didn't want Frank like that and she was sure about not turning him out. When he was about to nut she pushed him up off of her.

Then she said, "Just because you got the vagina doesn't mean nothing. So don't get your hopes up high or your feelings involved."

"I understand." Frank said. In Frank's reality, Tina was the finest woman he has ever had, with an added plus, her sex was good. After hanging for a while he walks Tina home. He tries to kiss her but she stops him.

"I told you Frank, we can only be friends."

"That's cool." Frank expresses with a hug. The New Year was moving along and on February 9th, 2003 Sheila decides to take her son to see Ice Man. He was looking well and his spirits were up. They talked and he asked his son all kinds of questions. He gave Sheila a drawing that he made for her. It was a Valentine's Day card. She tells him she loves it and embraces him with a hug. They talk until visiting hours were almost up. He hugs and tells them he loves them and goodbye. Sheila lets Ice Man know that she would be back soon with their son to see him. When Sheila got home she receives a call from Drew.

"Hey lady. Do you want to go to the club?"

"I would have to call you back." Sheila had to ask her mother if she would watch her son so she could go out. She agrees. She calls Drew back and informs him she can go. Later on he picks her up. Even though they had been going out for a while. Sheila still was not sure if she was ready for a commitment. At the club Sheila had a mixed drink and Drew had a beer. They sat at a table and began talking.

"Sheila we have been seeing each other for over a year now. I am ready for a commitment. I am tired of waiting and I want you to know that I love you."

"I understand. I am ready to move forward with you."

After they left the club they went back to Drew's place. He has a three-bedroom house with a big backyard. The two relax in the living room for a while and then they venture off into the bedroom. He lays Sheila on the bed. The room was dark. It has been a month since Drew had fucked Sheila and she was horny. He caresses her breast as he kisses her lips. Sheila pulls her jeans and panties off. Drew loved rubbing on Sheila's vagina because it was fat and hairy. He sticks his fingers inside of her tightness and then they get completely naked. He goes down eating her vagina. She was hot, wet and ready.

"I want you inside of me." Drew climbed on top of her and spread her legs. When he sticks his penis inside of her tight, wet vagina she clutches his back. He puts his entire shaft inside of her as she winds her hips throwing her vagina back at him.

"Is it good to you?" He asked.

"Yes baby, Fuck me." It was feeling so good to Sheila. She tells him to put her legs on his shoulders. Sheila liked being fucked hard. When he did what she asked, she starts screaming for more and then she bust. Drew turns her over and sticks it in from the back.

She hollers, "Oh baby!" He eases it out and gradually puts it back in. He spreads her ass cheeks and beats her vagina just the way she likes it. She loved it. He lays her on her side and raises her leg with his arm. Her vagina was real wet and filled with cum. Drew inserts himself back inside of her. After hitting her walls for a half an hour, he nuts inside of Sheila and then they take a shower together. Drew wanted Sheila to stay the night but she told him she needed to go home so she could get her son ready for church in the morning. He dropped her off at home and kisses her goodnight. Sheila had been going to church on the regular. When Sheila got up that morning she prepares breakfast for her family. She was in a good mood. Her mother and sister were getting ready for church. Her brother had gone off to the Navy. After they ate breakfast they went to church. Reverend Burch sermon was on living in sin. He started with husband's cheating on their wives and wives cheating on their husbands. He touched on people not being married and shacking up. Sheila began to wonder if Drew would marry her someday. She wanted her son to have a father figure in his life. After church Sheila went home and prepared dinner. Sheila's mother had only met Drew a few times during the course of them dating. She liked him because he was nice and respectful. Drew came over and ate dinner. They watch a little TV until it's time for Drew to go home and rest up for the work week. The next day while Sheila was at work she was talking to a co-worker about marriage. She was ready to settle down and give her son the life he deserves. She still loves Ice Man but she knew it was time to move on. Drew had become the perfect guy for her and he had won her heart. A few months later, Drew pops the question. He asked Sheila to marry him and to move in with him. She said yes. The following Saturday Sheila took her son to see Ice Man. She told him that Drew asked her for her hand in marriage and she said yes. Ice Man was hurt. He told her as long as Drew made her happy and he treats their son with respect, he could live with it. She let him know that from now on her mother would be bringing their son to see him. It was hard for him to accept the news but he understood. He stood up and gave her a hug and a kiss on the cheek. After the visit Ice Man went to his cell, lays down and cries. It was hard for him to let the past go. He knew he was the one that was supposed to marry Sheila. In June, Sheila and Drew got married and she and her son moved in with him. They were both very happy. They talked a lot about giving their lives back to Christ and raising her son in the church. They read the bible and prayed together as a family. Sheila and Drew love one another and it showed through the respect they shared. One day Sheila was sitting around and Tina crosses her mind. She had not seen her in a while and the last she heard she was still selling dope. She went by Grandma Mable's house one day and Grandma Mable was surprised to see her.

"Have you seen Tina? How is she doing?" Sheila asked.

"Tina is on drugs baby. I don't see her as much as I used to. But when she does come I will tell her you stopped by and asked about her." Sheila told Grandma Mable how she had changed her life and had gotten married. Grandma Mable could not believe it. She figured Sheila would have ended up with a house full of kids and on welfare. Sheila shows her wedding ring and Grandma Mable gives her a hug and lets her know how proud she was of her. As Sheila ready herself to leave, Grandma Mable reminds her to come back to see her anytime. Grandma Mable's sugar had gotten worse. She had to get both of her legs amputated and Tina did not even know. A week later Grandma Mable was rushed to the hospital because of her high sugar levels.

Chapter 21

Tina and Frank were still hanging in there rather tight. He fixed himself up a lot and slowed down on getting high. She even allowed Frank to have sex with her again. However, she would tell him every time not to allow his feelings to get involved. Frank had fallen in love with Tina and she didn't know. She felt a little something for him to but it wasn't love. Tina was still fucking Chuck and Chuck was still with his wife. Chuck wanted his cake and ice cream too. A couple of days later Chuck asked Tina to go to the club with him. It was a Friday night. Tina declined his invitation.

"Why?" Chucked inquired.

"I'm tired."

"Are you sleeping with Frank?"

With a serious look on her face, Tina replied, "No."

"Don't let me find out you are lying." Then Chuck hangs up. He was head over heels for Tina and he didn't want anybody fucking that but him. Tina went to visit Grandma Mable that Saturday morning. Her car was in the driveway but Tina did not get an answer at the door. She went to the next door neighbor's house and they let her know that Mable was at Carolina's Medical Center. Tina called a cab to surprise her but when she arrives, she was the one surprised. Her Grandmother was lying there with no legs. Tina began to cry. She reaches over and gives her Grandmother a hug and a kiss. She spent the whole day with her. Frank tried to call her but she didn't answer. Later that night after she returned home, she smoked some dope and told Sharon what was going on with her Grandmother. As she was fixing up another rock to smoke Frank was knocking at the door. As she stepped out the door to talk to him, Chuck pulls up. He calls Tina over to his jeep and asked, "Where have you been?" Tina was shell. Chuck got of his jeep.

"Have you been smoking dope?"

"No!" She screamed. Chuck threw her against the jeep and put his hands around her neck and commenced to choking her.

Frank ran up on Chuck. "Let Tina go." He said. Chuck smacked Frank and pulled out his pistol. Tina begs and cries for him not to shoot Frank. Chuck made Tina get in the jeep and drives off. Frank was left standing there alone. He was mad as hell. He took her down to the lake went down a path by some trees. Chuck was fired up. He smacks Tina in the mouth. "Bitch I thought you said you weren't fucking that nigga?"

Tina replies with tears streaming down her face, "I'm not."

He smacks her again. "Bitch don't make me kill you." She begs him not to hit her anymore. They sit in silence and then he pulls his penis out and makes her suck it. She was so nervous she didn't know what to do. She stroked it slowly as she pulls it towards her mouth. She put it as deep as it could go. She jacks it while she sucked on it and while Chuck was nutting, he grabs her head and presses it down as far as it could go as he nuts in her mouth. On the way back she said nothing. Frank was gone. When Chuck left Tina walks down to Frank's house. She knocks on his bedroom window and he comes to the backdoor.

"What's up Tina?"

She hugs him. "I am sorry for the commotion."

"I'm okay." Frank replied. "Come in for a while."

"No. I have to get home."

"Can I walk you home?"

"No." Tina replied.

"Will I see you tomorrow?" He asked.

"We have to cool it for a minute. Chuck threatened to kill me if he caught me with you again." The next day Chuck called Tina wanting to have sex with her. Tina was on her period and she was cramping like crazy. They talked about what happened and Chuck apologized to her. The following Saturday, Tina was selling dope all by herself. But she was still calling Frank. Later that night, two guys walk up to her and ask for two dimes. One of the guys hands her a $20 bill. As soon as she reaches for her stash, one of the guys pulls out a gun.

"Give it up," one of the guys said. The other guy takes her money and her pistol from her.

"Take the necklace and the ring off." Then they walked off as if nothing ever happened. Tina was mad as hell, mainly at Chuck, because he did not want Frank watching her back any longer. Tina went inside crying to Sharon about what had happened. She was about out of pocket. She calls Chuck and tells him what happened and he didn't believe her.

"You probably smoked it up." He said. She got mad and cursed him out. He hung up the phone on Tina. Tina was so upset. She smoked the rest of the dope and had $7 left to her name. The next morning, she went to Frank and told him what happened. He kissed her and told her that everything was going to be all right. They chill together for the rest of the evening. They even had sex. Later that night, Chuck was calling Tina but she would not answer his calls. Frank walked Tina home and gave her a hug and a kiss at the door. Chuck rode by and saw them. Tina was not able to recognize it was a mad Chuck, riding by because he was in his wife's car. He went down the street and turned around. When Frank left the yard towards home Chuck slowly rides pass and let his window down firing three shots that hit Frank in the side and chest. When Tina hears the shots she runs to the window and then Frank crosses her mind. She sees the little gray Honda speeding up the street fleeing the house. She runs out the door and looks up the street and sees someone lying on the ground. She runs towards the person and finds that it's Frank. She falls to her knees in tears. She fell to his aid crying even more. As blood runs from his mouth, Frank takes his last breath. Someone had already called for help. People had started gathering around. When help arrives they did everything they could to save Frank. At the hospital an investigator questions Tina. They asked her all kinds of questions. Did Frank sell dope? Did he have any enemies? She told them about the incident between Frank and Chuck and how Chuck had threatened to kill her if he saw her with him again. Then she tells them about the gray Honda Accord she saw. Two days later, Chuck was on the news for the murder of Frank. Tina was happy. A few days later Frank was laid to rest. She bought him some flowers for his grave. A week later Tina went to visit Grandma Mable. She had moved in with her sister and niece. She didn't look to good, but her spirits were always up when Tina came around. Tina didn't stay long. When she left Grandma remembers she didn't tell her about Sheila. The same day, Tina's cellphone was disconnected. She was feeling depressed. She went back to Sharon's and went to sleep. The next day she tried to get her old job back at the club but they would not hire her. She went to a couple of restaurants and grocery stores, but she still had no luck. She was so upset she went home. Later that night she took off walking. Tina wanted some dope. She ran into a guy and asked him if he knew where she could get some dope. He took her on Malibu Avenue and he coped three dimes. They walk back to his sister's house. They went in the backyard and he asked her what was up with her, she knew exactly what he wanted. She told him whatever. They got inside of an old Buick that was sitting in the back of the house. It was chilly outside so they smoked one bag.

"I can't fuck outside in this car. It's too cold" He went inside the house and brought out three blankets. He wrapped the blankets around them to keep them warm. He pulls out his penis and Tina sucks it for ten minutes. She asked him for a whole dime and he gives it to her. She smokes half and left the remainder for later. Tina pulls her pants down taking one leg out. She lays back and allows him to play with her vagina with his fingers. When his penis got hard he puts it inside of her. She rolls her lower half fast, tightening her muscles so that the guy could cum quick. And it worked. In 1 minute he was through. As Tina got dressed he asked her were would she be later because he had to pick up some money later on. She gave him the address and told him it was the only yellow house on the street. When Tina got home Sharon was knocked out with the door closed. Tina saw empty beer bottles in the trash and knew Sharon was tipsy. Tina went into her room and sat on the bed and began gazing out the window. About forty-five minutes the guy she had just fucked and sucked was at the door. He shows her the dope and she lets him in.

"You have to be quiet." Tina said. He gives her a bag to smoke. He didn't want to smoke. Tina gets naked and sits on the bed. She plays with his penis while she smokes the dope. He gives her another bag but she put it up. She sucks his penis until he was ready to take off his clothes. He inserts himself inside of her. He was good and hard this time and he felt comfortable with Tina. Tina was like, what the hell? She would give him his money's worth this time. He kisses Tina and rubs on her titties. Tina opens her legs wide for him. Her vagina was wet, as she rolls slowly inviting him deeper inside of her. After thirty minutes of fucking he bust a nut. He was still hard. Tina told him that was enough. He gave her another dime and she gave him a little more.

"Put me in the buck. I want to feel it and I want you to nut." He did and it didn't take long. She starts moaning as if it were hurting. When he was done Tina told him he had to leave and don't come back unless he had $50 in cash. She told him her vagina was too good to be giving it up for dope. Actually, she was trying to play him to see if he had more money. But he left. About a week later Tina found her a job as a cashier at Burger King. Everyday Tina would steal anywhere from $20-$30 to support her habit. She only worked 30 hours a week and made $5.75 an hour. Tina realizes that her period has not come on. She thought maybe it was normal because she'd been late before. That Thursday, Tina got fired. She got caught stealing money. The manager did not press charges but he told her not to ever come back in the restaurant again. It did not take her long, not even a day, Tina was back to selling her vagina. The next day she jumps in a car with a good-looking guy. He takes her to his house. When they got inside there was another man waiting. They sit at a table and he pulls out a package and gives her three dimes.

"You have to take care of me and my cousin." He said.

"Okay." She replied.

"Do you drink?"

"Yes." Tina said. He pours her a big glass of Vodka and water to chase it. After she smokes a bag and a half she tells him to come back into the room, while the cousin chills in the other room. She takes off her clothes and sits on the edge of the bed. He stands in front of her while she unzips his pants. She pulls his penis out and starts to suck it. When his penis got hard she knew it was going to hurt. He stuck his penis so deep in her throat, she gagged. Then he got naked. He pushes her up in the bed and sticks it in as he lifts her legs in the air. She moans as he plunges his penis in and out of her wet vagina. Then he lets her legs relax and fucks her some more.

"Bend over." He said. He beats her from the back for 15 minutes until he nuts inside of her. "I will be back in a few. I have to go drop a package off. Take care of my cousin and I will give you two more dimes when I get back." When he leaves, his cousin walks in the room looking at Tina stretched out naked.

"You are so pretty. Open your legs and let me look at your vagina?" She was so hairy and her vagina was wet and pink. When he got naked Tina could not believe what she was seeing. This guy had the biggest penis she had ever seen in her life. And it wasn't all the way hard. She didn't say a word. She just put it in her mouth. She used her tongue to tease the head of his penis and sucked it as she swiftly jacked it back in forth in and out of her mouth. She was going to try to make him cum quick once he got inside of her. Tina opens up as he straddles on top of her. He had to take it easy in order to put it inside of her. She was moving and telling him it hurt. When he got over half of it inside, he felt like he was tearing her insides up. Tina was screaming and crying. She scratches him on his back and he slaps her. He put her leg on his shoulder and forces it all inside of her. As he grabs her by her shoulders he looks down at tears streaming down her face.

"Please! Please! Get up." She begged. He fucked her for 30 minutes. She was so wet and it was so good to him he bust inside of her as well. When he took his penis out blood was running out of her vagina. He gave her a rag to put in her panties. She put on her clothes and sat back at the table and smoked the rest of her dope. Tina was in so much pain, but she cleaned the sheets that were on the bed. Once he finished washing up he came to the table where Tina was. He kisses Tina in the mouth and asked her to spend the night with him. When the other cousin returns, he took her home and gave her two more dimes. When she got home she went straight in the bathroom. When she sat down to pee a fetus dropped out in the toilet. She had gotten pregnant again and didn't even know it.

Chapter 22

She chilled for a couple of days. She hadn't been to see Grandma Mable. Grandma Mable was still not doing so well. A week later Tina was back on the block. She wanted to make some money to get high. A white man stops her and he wanted a blowjob. He gives her $20 and she hops in and took him to a dead end street. It didn't take her that long because she was that good. She bought two dimes and smoked it with some girl she didn't know. Then she walked around for an hour until she had another man that wanted her to jump in his car. And she did. He gave her $40 for sex. He took her to a motel and she fucked him for an hour and fifteen minutes. When he got through he dropped her back off. Tina went and bought her three dimes and went home. She gave Sharon $10 and gave her a dime and later that night she fucked and sucked five guys. The drugs had taken a toll on Tina. When she got in the next day she showered and ate. When she went to sleep she slept for two days. A few days later she ran into Suzie. She was riding with two dudes. They asked Tina if she wanted to go. So she hops in. They took the ladies to the Red Roof Inn. They got a room with double beds. Once they got in the room they had some drinks and smoked. They all got naked as they got high. The two guys fucked Tina and Suzie for hours. They switched up and after they finished the guys washed up. Tina liked the way one of the guys sexed her.

She even pulls him to the side and asked him, "What time are you coming back?"

"I don't know. But it will not be long."

"Can I chill until you get back?" Tina asked.

"Yes." He replied. When Suzie and the two guys left, Tina walks across the street to get her a Jr. Cheeseburger and some fries with the $2.50 she had in her pocket. After she ate she dozes off watching television. Two hours later, the two guys were back.

"Where is Suzie?"

"She left us." The guy that she had hollered at earlier told her not to worry about Suzie. He pulls out a half of eight, a 12-pack and a 5th of Night Train.

He gives Tina a piece of dope and said, "Let me see your body?" She stands up and gets naked. He pulls her towards him and starts playing with her vagina as she smiles at him.

"Sit down and get high." He said. He pours her some wine and passes her a beer. One of them was peeping out the window while the other guy was using the bathroom. Tina put a piece of dope that was lying in the floor in her pocket.

When he came out the bathroom he said, "Break time." He took his clothes off and pulls Tina to the bed. Then the other guy gets naked. While one was playing in her vagina the other was getting his penis sucked. They were fucking

Tina all types of ways. She was moaning but they were not hurting her that bad. Tina was horny and was actually enjoying it. She had gotten used to being fucked different kinds of ways. That was all she knew. And besides it had become her everyday living. When they finished the driver left. The guy she was feeling stayed. She fires up the piece of dope up she had kept with him and he did not say a thing. After they finish, she pushes him back to the bed. She kissing him in the mouth and throws her vagina on him. They fuck for hours. The next morning, she found a ride home. When she got in she went to sleep. Sharon was getting tired of Tina but she didn't want to throw her out in the streets. So she sat her down and had a talk with her. Tina went to visit Grandma Mable. Mable notices how much weight Tina was losing and how dark she had become in her face. Mable's sister knew Tina was on drugs. She told Tina that she needed to get her some help. But Tina was not trying to hear that. She loved the street life. Later when Tina left she ran into Suzie.

"Where are you going?" Tina asked her.

"I'm looking for a $40 piece." Tina walked with Suzie in the wee hours of the morning. The next morning Tina was feeling funny. She went to the health department and found out she had VD. She chilled for a few days and then she went back on the hoe stroll. She ran into a van full of guys one night. They asked her if she wanted to make some money and to get high. She was already jacked up, she didn't mind, she was down for anything. When she got in the van she observes five guys inside. They started feeling on Tina's titties and her vagina. They give her a snort of powder and asked her to show them her vagina.

She took her pants loose and pull them down. It had a little twain to it. But the guys didn't care. They were dope heads and they were ready to fuck. They pull up to a house and they all got out and went in. They gave Tina some dope to smoke and ran the train on her for hours. She was in so much pain, but all she wanted to do was get high. No matter how much pain it caused her. When they got through with Tina, they dropped her off on the Blvd. After a while another guy asked her if she wanted to get high. She agreed but not unless he got her a room. They went and got some dope and a room. He gave Tina a twenty-cent piece of crack. She smoked half of one and then got in the shower. When she came out Tina was naked and the guy liked what he saw. Even though she had lost a lot of weight, her body was still shapely with a nice little round ass. She lay back on the bed, as the guy got naked. He got on top of her telling her how sexy she was. He kisses her on the neck as he eases his penis inside of her. When he gets it all in, she rolls her hips. After a while he puts Tina on top of him. She rides his penis and he was enjoying it. Tina really knew how to fuck. They took a break and got high some more. Tina was tired. When they got through the guy left Tina so she could get some sleep. He told her he would come back later. Tina fell asleep. Later that night he came back with burgers and fries. He woke her up and gave her the food from McDonald's. While she ate they had conversation.

"Why are you on the streets?" He asked her.

"It's life." When she got through eating they got high. Then he fucked her again. They were woken up by room service letting them know it was check out time.

They left. When Tina got home Sharon was leaving with her sister. She was taking her to pay some bills. Tina went in her room. It was getting dark when Sharon got back home from seeing her mother with her sister. Tina was still sleep, so Sharon did not bother her. A couple weeks later on a Thursday, Sharon told Tina she had to find her somewhere else to live. Tina asked if she could give her until tomorrow. It was Friday, March 12, 2003 and Tina gathered some of her clothes and left. When she got on the Blvd a guy picked her up and took her back to his place. He fucked her for a few hours then he dropped her back off. Later that night she saw a lady walking pass her hollering at a car.

Tina looked back at her and said, "Strawberry is that you?"

"Yes."

"I'm Tina, B-Money's old girl." They hug and sit down at a bus stop. They talk about the past and how B-Money treated them. Then Strawberry told Tina how she was robbed and beat after she left town with B-Money's dope and money.

"I have nowhere to go."

"I will catch up with you later. You can stay with me." Strawberry jumps in a car leaving Tina sitting at the bus stop. A car pulls up with a Latino man inside. Tina gets in and goes to his apartment. The man lets her know he only has $25.

"I will take that." She said. While they were taking off their clothes she tells him not to hurt her. He sits on the couch as she sucks his penis.

He tells her, "That's enough." He gradually sticks his penis inside of her. She squirms a little but he didn't try to hurt her. She liked that because most guys tried to take advantage of her. When he got through he gives her a hug and thanks her and then drops her back off on the Blvd. She walks around looking for dope she had no luck in finding. About 30 minutes later she runs into Strawberry.

"Strawberry where can I find some dope? I have $25."

"I have $30." They walk towards Breech Avenue to a house Strawberry is familiar with. Tina stays outside while Strawberry goes in. A drunken man walks up and asked Tina to fuck for $10. Tina said no. By this time Strawberry was coming out the door.

"Tina I stay with an old man and he likes to get drunk. He wouldn't even know you are living there." It took them 20 minutes before they got to the house. They couldn't wait to smoke. Strawberry had a key to the house. When they got in Pops was asleep on the couch.

They go into another room and Strawberry asked Tina, "Where have you been staying?"

"Anywhere I could lay my head down." They got high and Strawberry pours them some Vodka that Pops had. He kept him a half of a gallon in the house. After they got high, they talked until they fell asleep. The next day Strawberry gave Tina some clothes to wear. She fixed them something to eat while they catch up more in conversation.

"A lot of my clothes I take off people's clothes line. You have to steal sometimes when you are out here getting high." Tina laughed but she knew Strawberry was telling the truth. Pops woke up and sees Tina.

"Strawberry who is this fine young lady?"

"This is my sister Tina." When she finished cooking she prepares their lunch. They ate and had a few drinks and Strawberry tells Tina, "I will catch you later. I have to go get me something to smoke."

"Me too." Tina said as she grabs her jacket. For the next couple of weeks, the girls did what they did best. They both stayed high. When one didn't have the other made sure they did. They had become close. They were becoming a team. Tina was beginning to fit in. Pops liked her. She would even tease him. She would ask him to take his penis out and let her feel it, and he would. He gave them money sometimes but the ladies made their own money most of the time. One night after getting high in the middle of April, Tina asked Strawberry if she wanted to sell some dope. She stares at Tina like she was crazy. Tina lets her know that she is tired of selling her vagina and she was ready to get back on. She had come up with a plan. Tina told Strawberry how they could sell their vagina to come up with the money to buy the package.

"Are you serious?" Strawberry asked. "This will not work because we both smoke." Tina knew she could do it because she knew how to hustle.

"That's when you have to be strong. All we have to do is let the girls know on the block that we got dope and where we will be."

It sounds good. But could we really do this?"

"Yes! Trust me…tomorrow…Friday night and the Blvd is going to be busy with men who want dates. We only fucking for $30 or more. No dope! We save all the money and put it together and get a package." Thursday night they inform the girls on the block that there was going to be some good dope at 3720 Breech Avenue tomorrow night. Then they went their way. Tina got in the house early. It was slow and she didn't feel like sucking and fucking. Strawberry got in about 11:30 with three dimes. Before they got high Tina told her, "Remember tomorrow is all business, no play. We can do this my sister." They got high and chilled for the rest of the night.

Chapter 23

Friday morning, the ladies ate breakfast and then showered and got dressed. Tina was serious when she tells Strawberry, "Whatever money you make, put it in your sock and save it." Tina was so determined to get back on, she could feel it. They left the house before noon. When they reach the Blvd a car stops and it was two guys that wanted sex for dope.

Tina looks at Strawberry and said, "No. We have to be strong and we will have our own package a little later on." Five minutes later, a white guy pulls up and Tina hops in. She tells Strawberry to meet her back at the house at 7:00 PM and to not be late. Strawberry flags a van down and gets in. Tina arrives back at Pop's house at 6:30 AM. She made $95.00. About 7:05 AM, Strawberry walks in and pulls out $75. Tina gives her a hug.

"I knew you could do it girl." Then they leave to go on Breech Avenue. A guy named John comes to the door.

"Do you have an eight ball?" Tina asked.

"Yeah," he said as he walks into another room. When he came back with the package Tina hands him $140 and then they leave. On the way back they stop at the corner store to get some sandwich bags, food, wine and beer and head back home. They offer Pops a beer and go in the room to bag up the dope. Once they finish they head to the Blvd. They give a few of the girls on the block a taste. They tell Tina that the dope was good and Tina told them where to come to get more. They made a few sells and then head back home. They smoke a bag together and downed some beer and wine until one of the girls they knew off the streets came by with a guy for four dimes. Another customer came and she wanted three. Throughout the night people were coming back to back for dope. They had gotten word from the girls on the Blvd that the dope was good and they were up all night long. By 8 AM they had doubled their money. They went to sleep and woke up Saturday afternoon. They showered and went back to see John and then off to the Blvd. Tina knew how to hustle. She sold dope while she walked around.

She told Strawberry, "Just watch my back." When they got back home they bagged up some more dope. Within a month's time, they were booming out of Pop's place. They were selling and smoking dope. But Tina knew how to make sure they maintained. Tina had bought them both clothes and some jewelry. They had the girls from the Blvd bringing them plenty of business and Tina gave them an extra bag at times. After people in the neighborhood started coming she had the foot traffic coming to the back door. Tina and Strawberry fell back on getting high during the daytime. They had to be alert just in case the jump out van came through. They let their customers know that after 2 AM no dope will be sold. It was slow on a Wednesday evening. Tina had just bought an ounce from John. Tina, Pops and Strawberry sat around and drank all night long, until Pops fell out. Tina fixed up a rock for her and

Strawberry and they continued drinking. Strawberry went into the room and took all her clothes off and lay down in the bed. Tina followed behind her. She took off her clothes and put on her sexy lingerie.

She sat on the bed and said, "Strawberry, have you ever been with another woman before?"

"What do you mean by that?" Tina kissed Strawberry on the lips and rubs her vagina.

"What are you doing?" Strawberry said.

"What does it look like?" Tina pulls Strawberry's panties to the side and sticks her fingers in her vagina. Neither of the ladies had been with a guy in a while. They had been too busy selling dope and getting high. And it didn't bother them one bit. As Tina moves her fingers around inside of Strawberry, she opens up her legs and closes her eyes. Tina licks her vagina with slow gentle strokes. Strawberry did not know what to think about Tina. All she knew, is that it felt good to her and she did not want Tina to stop. Tina put a third finger inside of her while she sucked her clit. Strawberry pulls Tina up off of her because she was about to nut.

"Suck my titties and put your fingers back inside of me so I can cum?"

"Sit on my face and eat my vagina while I eat yours?" Tina said. They did the 69. Strawberry nutted all on Tina's fingers, then they got up to wash up.

"Tina why did you want to do that?" Tina told her about the relationship she had with Sara and that she wanted to be with another woman. Neither one of them had a man so they agreed to fuck each other when the time came. The next day, Tina went out and bought a dildo and for the rest of the day she and Strawberry chilled. Word got back to them that John had gotten busted. That Thursday night they had no other choice but to close up shop. By Friday night, they were sold out. Tina found a new contact. She started buying dope from Big Rob. He had wanted to fuck Tina for a while. One day she went to get some dope from him and he tried to crack on her. She said no and left. He told some of his friends that were in the house how fine Tina used to be and let one of the guys know that he wanted to fuck her friend Strawberry. When Tina got in, Strawberry was asleep so she bagged up the dope herself. They sold the ounce in a day. Tina was tired and she needed some rest. She sent Strawberry to go buy the dope from Big Rob. When she got there Big Rob started cracking on Strawberry. Strawberry asked him for a ride. He did it because he felt she was interested in him.

When they got to the house Big Rob asked Strawberry, "Do you have a man?"

"Tina is my man." He looked surprised.

"If you want some real penis holler at me." Tina was looking out the door as Strawberry hops out the car with a smile on her face. Tina gave her the evil eye when she enters the house.

"Don't even think about it." Strawberry said.

"We need a used car." Tina said. After they finished bagging the dope Tina remembered that her Grandmother still had her 82 Oldsmobile at her aunt's house in the backyard. Nothing was wrong with it and no one was using it. All it needed was insurance and a battery. Plus, she hadn't seen Grandma Mable in a month and a half. The next morning Tina went to visit her grandmother. She told Tina that she could have the car. She signed the title over to her and Tina went to get it notarized. The next day she got the insurance and tag for the car. When she got back home Strawberry was gone. But the dope was still in the hiding spot. She sat and talked to Pops, who was drunk. People started coming by for dope and Tina was doing it alone. When Strawberry finally came in, her and Tina got into an argument. She told Tina she was not trying to hear it and jumps in the bed. Tina was so hot she gets in the shower. About five minutes later a butt naked Strawberry had joined her. They washed each other's bodies while they talked their problems out. When they finished they went to bed. While fixing breakfast Tina talked to Strawberry about going to the club. Tina had not been in a while. It was Friday night so they decided to go out. She didn't drink much, but Strawberry sure did. She danced with everybody. Tina knew it was time to go home. When they got in Strawberry wanted Tina to sex her. Tina did not want to be bothered. A week later Tina gave Strawberry some money to get some dope from Big Rob. Tina had to go back over to Carolinas Medical Center because Grandma Mable had gotten sick again. Strawberry drops her off at the hospital and heads over to Big Rob's. He was there alone looking at a sex tape. He told her it would be a while before he got some dope. Strawberry told him she had time to wait. He fires up a blunt and fixes her a drink.

"Where is Tina?"

"Visiting her Grandmother at the hospital." After they smoked the blunt he asked Strawberry, "Can I have some vagina?"

"Okay. Let's go." He takes her to his room and they get butt naked. She sucks his penis until he was ready to lay her down. He sticks his fingers in her vagina and sucks on her titties. He got between her legs and stuck his penis inside of her. Strawberry moaned a little. She fucked him back.

"Oooohhh this feels so good Rob."

Chapter 24

A couple of months later nothing much changed and Strawberry was still fucking Big Rob. It was two nights before Christmas and Strawberry sneaks on the phone and calls Big Rob.

"I want to come and see you."

"Okay, Come on." Tina and Strawberry had been smoking and drinking and then the argument started. Strawberry needed an excuse to get out the house so she could go see Big Rob. Tina told her to go to bed. But she wouldn't. Tina on the other hand went into the room and goes to bed. Strawberry took all the money and the dope. She didn't want anything else to do with Tina. She wanted to be with Big Rob. She didn't know how to tell Tina. So she left. She took Tina's car keys off the dresser and left. It had been snowing and sleeting all day. She got in the car and took off towards Big Rob's. She was so high she didn't realize how fast she was driving. A block away from his house, she runs off the road and hits a tree. She was ejected through the windshield and died instantly. When the ambulance got on the scene Big Rob was walking towards the wreck. He recognizes the car and then he says, Strawberry. He could not believe his eyes. He stood back, helplessly watching what had unfolded. The police found the dope hanging out of her pockets and money on the seat. They ran the license tag and an officers was sent to Pop's house. They questioned Tina and then they let her know that Strawberry was dead. Tina cried as she told them that she had been sleep all night and she must have stolen her car. Tina really didn't know what she was going to do now. Strawberry's body was taken to Florida where her mother lived. Tina did not attend the funeral. The New Year had come and Tina was back to her old self. She had turned Pop's house into a whorehouse. She fucked and sucked as many types of men for dope that she could. On the 3rd of the month she would even suck Pop's penis for money. One night while Pops was asleep Tina brought a man in and took him in the room. When she asked him for the money he pulls out a gun and tells her to shut up and take her clothes off. He made her suck his penis and then he bent her over and hit her from the back for hours. Then he left her on the bed. During this time Tina had lost a lot of weight. Her skin was dark and her hair was thinning out. She woke up many times during the night drenched in sweat. Tina was sleeping around with women and men for dope. She had to have it, no matter what she had to do. She cleaned herself one morning and went over to Grandma's old house. A lady that knew Tina told her she was sorry to hear about Mable. Tina had no idea at what she was talking about.

Then the lady asked, "When is the funeral?"

Tina started crying. "Is my Grandma dead?" The woman thought Tina knew.

"Yes baby. She died two days ago." Tina got the woman to take her over to her Aunt's house. They told her that they had been looking for her. She stayed long enough for them to buy her an outfit for the funeral. After Grandma Mable was buried Tina left for the streets again. Sheila and her husband were getting along well. She didn't even know that Mable had passed away. She had another child with Drew. This time she had a girl. She was one-years-old now. One Saturday, Sheila decided to take her to see Ice Man. On the way home she stops by Mable's house. A neighbor informed her that she had passed away. When she got home she thought about Tina and all the fun they used to have. She was now ready to make amends with Tina. When Drew came in from shooting ball he asked Sheila if she wanted to go out to dinner. She agrees and they took the kids out for a sit down dinner. That Saturday night Tina was beaten and raped by three white guys. She lay in an abandon building with a bruised face. After church that Sunday, God had put it on Sheila's heart to go and find Tina. She rode around for hours until someone told her where Tina hung out. It started to rain as she was driving down the Blvd. She took a left on Spencer Ave. As she got smoothly around the curve a lady was walking. She pulls over and jumps out the car and screamed, "Tina!" The lady looks back. It was Tina. Tina briskly walks towards Sheila with tears in her eyes. Sheila could not believe how bad Tina looks and smells. But she hugs her as they cry in each other's arms. Sheila took Tina home with her and allows her to bathe. She provides her some clothes and something to eat. Then they went out on the porch to talk. They talked about everything.

"Tina I forgave you a long time ago for having sex with Ice-Man. I knew it was the drugs. God has changed my life and I got married to Drew." She allowed Tina to spend the night and talked her into going to Charlotte's Detox Clinic the next morning. When Tina checked in, Sheila gave her the phone number, money and some snacks. She told Tina she was going to buy her clothes and bring it back to her tomorrow. She kissed her on the cheek and said, "Girl I love you. It's going to be alright." That week Tina was sick and went to the hospital and later brought back to Detox. She stayed there for two weeks and then she entered a halfway house on the bus line. So she could make her morning meetings, Tina found her a job at the Waffle House working 2nd shift. A month later she started working mornings and was making her meetings at night. One night at a meeting a lady came up to her and gave her a hug. She pulled her shades off and its Linda.

"Welcome home stranger." And gave her another hug. Tina was glad to see Linda. She had not seen her in years. After the meeting Linda told Tina how long she had been clean and how good she was doing. Tina had only been clean for a couple of months. She asked Linda if she would sponsor her and she said yes. When she was 9 months clean she went to the health department. She wanted to find out why she had loss so much weight. Even though she had normal eating habits. She heard a woman sharing at a meeting on how she found out she had AIDS.

Chapter 25

A week later Tina went back for her results. She found out she was HIV positive. She had it for a while. She cried in the doctor's office. He counseled her and ordered more blood work to determine what medications she would have to take. Tina was counseled and referred out for counseling to help her cope with the news. Tina was now celebrating her one-year anniversary. Linda and Sheila and her family came to support and celebrate her. Linda presented her with her one-year medallion. After the meeting, Sheila and her family took her out to dinner. Later that night, Tina called Sheila to let her know that she was HIV positive. Sheila was hurt. She asked Tina was she okay. Tina told her she didn't know. Tina kept attending her meetings and she never gave up. She called Linda one night and asked her if she could tell her story in the home group. On January 17, 2005 Tina got the chance to tell her story. At first she was a little nervous. Linda told her that it was normal to feel this way.

"That's just God shaking the truth out of you." At the beginning of the meeting Linda introduced Tina to the group as the speaker. She got up and went to the front of the room.

"Hey. My name is Tina. First of all, I thank my higher power for allowing me to be here. And if you are a new comer, keep coming back, no matter what. You never ever have to use drugs again. I was born here in Charlotte. My mother died when I was young and my father was sent to prison when I was six years old. I never got the chance to know him or my mother. I met my father's sister and her son when I got older. I was raised by my Grandma, who raised me the best way she could. I never wanted for anything. She was a very sweet person and she gave me a lot of love and support. I started cheerleading in junior high school. After high school I started drinking, smoking pot and partying. Then I started having sex. I enjoyed it. after a while, I started dating a dope dealer for five years and he was killed. In that relationship I started selling drugs and I got hooked on crack. Then he became abusive and he even beat a baby out of me. Later at his funeral I found out he was my first cousin. I got deeper in the game when I got strung out. I loved the money, getting high and the fast life. I started sleeping around with all types of people for money. I even slept with women. My very first girlfriend was raped and killed in a park. I dated another woman who died in a car crash from driving drunk. We got in an argument one night and she stole my car. I didn't get to tell neither one of them how much I loved them. I stood on the street corners all times of the day and night prostituting my body. I stole from my Grandma and other people. I have been beaten and raped numerous times. But I was caught up in the game. Till I thought there was no way out. I felt alone. Everyone I loved and who loved me is gone. But I thank God for my new family. You, the people of NA for saving my life. Today I know I have a choice and that's to live or die using drugs. I want to live a clean life and I don't want to die using drugs. I found out a while back that I was HIV positive but I don't let that keep me from making my meetings. My life is not over with yet. I wish I could turn back the hands of times. But I can't. I feel like there is nothing I can do today but take my medicine and live. I look around this room and I see a lot of young people in here. Stay, keep coming back, no matter what. You never ever have to use dope again because there is hope without dope. It's called Narcotics Anonymous. Thank you for letting me share." A year had gone by and Tina had managed to stay clean. She kept attending her meetings and going to church. She also gave her life to Christ. Her and Sheila had gotten closer than ever. One night, Sheila received a call from the hospital. She rushed right over. Tina's immune system had broken down. She had pneumonia again and was very frail. She had loss about 75 pounds. The doctors told Sheila there was nothing else they could do for her. Sheila talked Drew into allowing Tina to live with them. The next morning, they picked Tina up from the hospital. Sheila knew what she would have to go through taking care of Tina. But she refused to let her die alone. Sheila took a month off from work. She explained the situation to her manager. It was hard for Sheila seeing Tina lay there in her condition. One night she heard Tina moan. She rushes in the room and turns on the light and sits on the bed beside Tina. Sheila grabs Tina's hand and tears flows from Tina's eyes as she took her last breath. Sheila screams as she looks at Tina.

Drew runs into the room and held Sheila as she cried, "She is dead." She told him the time of death as he called 911. The day of Tina's funeral a lot of people showed up. Some talked good about her. Sheila sung 'Precious Lord'. As they were taking her body to the cemetery Sheila thought about all the things they had been through. When her casket was lowered into the ground, Sheila started crying. She felt like she had lost her sister.

Tina went to meetings for as long as she could. She died February 6, 2006 at the age of 36. Today we still have Tina's running around. So please talk to your sons and daughters. Let them know the risk they take when dealing with sex and drug.